"Exactly when did the stove catch on fire?"

The panicked blonde pushed back a lock of hair. "About five minutes after I turned it on. I was just trying to make tea."

Why did he have to find out the cottage he'd intended to buy had been sold this way? He forced kindness into his tone. "Don't ever hesitate to call on us, Charlotte. But why the sudden need for tea?"

She flushed. "I just signed the papers on the place today. I told Melba I just wanted to have a cup of tea on my new deck."

"You're Melba's friend?"

Chief Bradens had mentioned his wife's friend was buying a weekend cottage in town. Now, annoyed as he was, he'd have to be nice. A friend of the fire chief's wife demanded special care. Jesse pulled a business card from his pants pocket. "I'm a licensed contractor. If you like, I'll help you figure out what really needs work." If he couldn't have the house, maybe he could at least get the work.

She narrowed her eyes. "Why would you do that?"

"Because you're a friend of the chief's. Because I'm a nice guy." *Because I'm trying not to be a sore loser.*

Books by Allie Pleiter

Love Inspired

My So-Called Love Life
The Perfect Blend
*Bluegrass Hero
*Bluegrass Courtship
*Bluegrass Blessings
*Bluegrass Christmas
Easter Promises
  *"Bluegrass Easter"
†Falling for the Fireman
†The Fireman's Homecoming
†The Firefighter's Match
†A Heart to Heal
†Saved by the Fireman

Love Inspired Historical

Masked by Moonlight
Mission of Hope
Yukon Wedding
Homefront Hero
Family Lessons
The Lawman's Oklahoma Sweetheart

Love Inspired Single Title

Bad Heiress Day
Queen Esther &
  the Second Graders of Doom

*Kentucky Corners
†Gordon Falls

ALLIE PLEITER

Enthusiastic but slightly untidy mother of two, RITA®
Award finalist Allie Pleiter writes both fiction and
nonfiction. An avid knitter and unreformed choco-
holic, she spends her days writing books, drinking
coffee and finding new ways to avoid housework. Allie grew up in Connecticut, holds a B.S. in speech
from Northwestern University and spent fifteen
years in the field of professional fund-raising. She
lives with her husband, children and a Havanese dog
named Bella in the suburbs of Chicago, Illinois.

Saved by the Fireman

Allie Pleiter

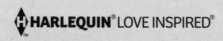

Recycling programs
for this product may
not exist in your area.

™ LOVE INSPIRED BOOKS

ISBN-13: 978-0-373-87922-9

Saved by the Fireman

www.Harlequin.com

Printed in U.S.A.

Unless the Lord builds the house, the builders labor in vain. Unless the Lord watches over the city, the guards stand watch in vain.
—*Psalms* 127:1

To Abbie
In faith that she'll discover many wonderful directions

Chapter One

Charlotte Taylor sat in her boss's office Friday morning and wondered where all the oxygen in Chicago had just gone.

"I'm sorry to let you go, Charlotte, I really am." Alice Warren, Charlotte's superior at Monarch Textiles, looked genuinely upset at having to deliver such news. "I know you just lost your grandmother, so I tried to put this off as long as I could."

A layoff? Her? Charlotte felt the shock give way to a sickening recognition. She'd seen the financial statements; she'd written several of the sales reports. Sure, she was no analyst wiz, but she was smart enough to know Monarch wasn't in great financial shape and a downsize was likely. She was also emotionally tied enough to Monarch and torn enough over losing Mima that she'd successfully denied the company's fiscal health for months. As she watched her grandmother's decline, Charlotte told herself she was finally settled into a good life. She'd boasted to a failing Mima—not entirely truthfully, she knew even then on some level—about feeling "established."

She'd patted Mima's weakening hands, those hands

that had first taught her to knit and launched the textile career she had enjoyed until five minutes ago, and she'd assured her grandmother that there was no reason to worry about her. She was at a place in life where she could do things, buy things, experience things and get all the joy out of life just as Mima taught her. How hollow all that crowing she had done about becoming "successful" and "indispensable" at Monarch now rang. Who was she fooling? In this economy, did anyone really have the luxury of being indispensable?

Except maybe Mima. Mima could never be replaced. Charlotte and her mother were just barely figuring out how to carry on without the vivacious, adventurous old woman who'd now left such a gaping hole in their lives. It had been hard enough when Grandpa had lost his battle to Alzheimer's—the end of that long, hard decline could almost be counted as a blessing. Mima's all-too-quick exit had left Charlotte reeling, fabricating stability and extravagance that were never really there. Hadn't today just proved that?

Charlotte grappled for a response to her boss's pained eyes. "It's not your fault, I suppose." She was Monarch's problem solver, the go-to girl who never got rattled. She should say something mature and wise, something unsinkably optimistic, something Mima would say. Nothing came but a silent, slack jaw that broadcast to Alice how the news had knocked the wind out of her.

Alice sighed. "You know it's not your performance. It's just budgetary. I'm so sorry."

"The online sales haven't been growing as fast as we projected. I'd guessed the layoffs were coming eventually. I just didn't think it'd be—" she forced back the lump in her throat "—me, you know?"

Alice pulled two tissues from the box on her desk,

handing one to Charlotte. "It's not just you." She sniffed. "You're the first of four." She pushed an envelope across the desk to Charlotte. "I fought for a severance package, but it's not much."

A severance package. Charlotte didn't even want to open it. Whatever it included, the look on Alice's face told Charlotte it wasn't going to make much of a difference. *Mima, did you see this coming?* Of course that couldn't be possible, but Charlotte felt her grandmother's eyes on her anyway, watching her from the all-knowing viewpoint of eternity. It wasn't that much of a stretch, if one believed in premonitions. Or the Holy Spirit, which Mima claimed to listen to carefully.

In true Mima style, Charlotte's grandmother had left both her and her mother a sizable sum of money and with instructions to "do something really worth doing." A world traveler after Grandpa died, Mima squeezed every joy out of life and was always encouraging others to do the same. Mima bought herself beautiful jewelry but never cried when a piece got lost. Mima owned a ten-year-old car but had visited five continents. She bought art—real art—but had creaky old furniture. Her apartment was small but stuffed with fabulous souvenirs and wonderful crafts. Mima truly knew what money was for and what really mattered in life.

That was how Charlotte knew the funds she'd inherited weren't intended for living—rent and groceries and such—they were for dreams and art and *life*. Having to use Mima's money to survive a layoff would feel like an insult to her grandmother's memory.

Alice sniffled, bringing Charlotte back to the horrible conversation at hand. Alice was so distressed she seemed to fold in on herself. "I wasn't allowed to tip anyone off. I'm so sorry."

She was sorry—even Charlotte could see that—but it changed nothing. Charlotte was leaving Monarch. She'd been laid off from the job she'd expected to solidify her career. It felt as if she'd spent her four years at Monarch knitting up some complicated, beautiful pattern and someone had come and ripped all the stitches out and told her to start over.

Over? How does a person start over when they suddenly doubt they ever really started at all?

Charlotte picked up the envelope but set it in her lap unopened.

"You've got two weeks of salaried work still to go." Alice was trying—unsuccessfully—to brighten her voice. "But you've also got six days of vacation accrued so…you don't have to stay the whole two weeks if you don't want to." The woman actually winced. Was this Alice's kinder, gentler version of "clean out your desk"?

The compulsion to flee roared up from some dark corner of her stomach Charlotte didn't even know she had. She didn't want to stay another minute. The fierce response surprised her—Monarch had been so much of a daily home to her she often didn't think of it as work. "And what about sick days?"

It bothered Charlotte that Alice had evidently anticipated that question; she didn't even have to look it up. "Two."

She was better than this. She couldn't control that she was leaving, but she could control when she left. And that was going to be now. "I don't think I'm feeling so well all of a sudden." Sure, it was a tad unreasonable, but so was having your job yanked out from underneath you. She had eight covered days out of her two-week notice. What was the point of staying two more days? Two more hours? Her files were meticulous, her sales contact software completely up to date, and next season's catalogue was ahead of schedule. There wasn't a single thing keeping her here except the time it would take to sweep all the personal decorations from her desk.

Alice nodded. "I'll write you a glowing recommendation."

It felt like such a weak compensation. Charlotte stood up, needing to get out of this office where she'd been told so many times—and believed—she was a gifted marketing coordinator and a key employee. "Thanks." She couldn't even look Alice in the eye, waving goodbye with the offending manila envelope as she walked out the door.

Monarch only had two dozen or so employees, and every eye in the small office now stared at her as she packed up her desk. Charlotte was grateful each item she stuffed into one of the popular Monarch tote bags— and oh, the irony of that—transformed the damp surge of impending tears into a churning burst of anger. Suddenly the sweet fresh-out-of-college intern she'd been training looked like the enemy. Inexperience meant lower salaries, so it wouldn't surprise Charlotte at all if adorable little Mackenzie got to keep her job. She probably still lived at home with her parents and didn't even need money for rent, Charlotte thought bitterly.

She reached into her file drawer for personal papers, her hand stilling on the thick file labeled "Cottage." The file was years old, a collection of photos and swatches and magazine articles for a dream house. Apartment living had its charms, but with Charlotte's craft-filled background, she longed to have a real house, with a yard and a front porch and windows with real panes. One that she could decorate exactly the way she wanted.

Just last week, Charlotte had nearly settled on using

Mima's funds to buy a cottage in nearby Gordon Falls. It would be too far for a daily commute, but she could use it on weekends and holidays. She knew so many people there. Her best friend, Melba, had moved there. Her cousins JJ and Max had moved there. Melba's new baby, Maria, was now Charlotte's goddaughter. She'd come to love the tiny little resort town three hours away on the Gordon River, and there was a run-down cottage she'd driven past dozens of times that Charlotte could never quite get out of her mind. Mima would approve of her using the money to fund an absolutely perfect renovation in a town where everyone seemed to find happiness.

Well, not now, Charlotte thought as she stuffed the file into the bag. In light of the past five minutes, a weekend place had gone from exciting to exorbitant. *Get out of here before you can't hold it in,* she told herself as she stuffed three framed photos—one of Mom, one of Mima and one of baby Maria—in beside the thick file. She zipped the tote bag shut with a vengeance, yanked the employee identification/security badge from around her neck and set it squarely in the middle of the desk. Just last week she'd bought a beautifully beaded lariat to hold the badge, but now the necklace felt as if it was choking her. She left it along with the badge, never wanting to see it again.

With one declarative "I may be down but I'm not out" glare around the office, Charlotte left, not even bothering to shut the door behind her.

Jesse Sykes flipped the steak and listened to the sizzle that filled one end of his parents' patio. He'd built this outdoor kitchen two years ago, and this grill was a masterpiece—the perfect place to spend a Saturday afternoon. He planned to use a photo of the fire pit on his business brochures once they got printed. That, and the portico his mother loved. Filled with grapevines that turned a riot of gorgeous colors in the fall, it made for a stunning graphic. Only two more months, and he'd have enough funds to quit his job at Mondale Construction, buy that little cottage on the corner of Post and Tyler, fix it up and flip it to some city weekender for a tidy profit. With that money, he'd start his own business at last.

Move-in properties were plucked up quickly in Gordon Falls, so finding the perfect fixer-upper was crucial. He'd already lost out on two other houses last fall because he didn't quite have the down payment stashed away, but the cottage he'd settled on now was perfect. It was June, and he'd planned to buy the place in March, but that was life. He'd needed a new truck and Dad sure wasn't going to offer any help in that department. A few months' delay shouldn't make a difference, though—the cottage had been on the market for ages. It needed too much renovation for most people to want to bother.

"I'm pretty sure I'll have Sykes Homes Incorporated up and running by the fall. I can still snag the fall colors season if I can buy that cottage."

Dad sat back in his lawn chair, eyes squinting in that annoying way Jesse knew heralded his father's judgment. "Fall? Spring is when they buy. Timing is everything, son. You've got to act fast or you lose out on the best opportunities, and those won't be around in September."

Jesse flipped the next steak. "I'm moving as fast as I can, Dad." As if he didn't know he'd missed the spring season. As if it hadn't already kept him up nights even more than the Gordon Falls Volunteer Fire Department alarms.

"It might not be fast enough."

Jesse straightened his stance before turning to his father. "True, but learning to adapt is a good lesson, too. This won't be the first time I've had to retool a plan because I've hit a hitch."

Dad stood up and clamped a hand on Jesse's shoulder. "Son, all you've hit is hitches so far." This time he didn't even bother to add the false smile of encouragement he sometimes tacked on to a slam like that. Jesse thrust his tines into the third steak and clamped his teeth together.

"Is it that older cottage on Post Avenue?" his mother asked. "The one by the corner with the wrought-iron window boxes?"

The wrought-iron window boxes currently rusting out of their brackets and splitting the sills, yes. "That's it."

He caught the "leave him be" look Mom gave Dad as she came over and refilled Jesse's tall glass of iced tea. "Oh, I like that one. So much charm. I've been surprised no one's snatched it up since Lucinda Hyatt died. You'll do a lovely job with that."

"In two more months I'll be ready to make an offer."

"You could have had the money for it by now if it weren't for the firehouse taking up all your time. You have no salary to show for it and it keeps you away from paying work. You'd better watch out or this place will be sold out from underneath you like the last one, and you'll be working for Art Mondale for another five years." Dad's voice held just enough of a patronizing tone to be polite but still drive the point home.

"Mike, don't let's get into that again."

Dad just grunted. Jesse's place in the volunteer fire department had been a never-ending battle with his father. Jesse loved his work there, loved helping people. And by this point, he felt as if the firefighters were a second family who understood him better than his real one. Chief Bradens was a good friend and a great mentor, teaching Jesse a lot about leadership and life. Fire Inspector Chad Owens had begun to teach him the ins and outs of construction, zoning and permits, too. It was the furthest thing he could imagine from the waste of time and energy his father obviously thought it to be.

Mom touched Jesse's shoulder. "You're adaptable. You can plot your way around any obstacle. That's what makes you so good at the firehouse."

Jesse hoisted the steaks onto a platter his mother held out. "That, and my world-class cooking." Then, because it was better to get all the ugliness out before they started eating, Jesse made himself ask, "How come Randy isn't here?"

Dad's smirk was hard to ignore. "Your brother's at a financial conference in San Diego this week. He said it could lead to some very profitable opportunities." Jesse's younger brother, Randall, would be retiring in his forties if he kept up his current run of financial success. Randy seemed to be making money hand over fist, boasting a fancy condo in the Quad Cities, a travel schedule that read more like a tourist brochure, and a host of snazzy executive trappings. It didn't take a genius to see Jesse fell far short of his brother in Dad's eyes. A month ago, when Jesse had pulled up to the house in a brand-new truck, Jesse couldn't help but notice the way his father frowned at it, parked next to Randy's shiny silver roadster.

"He's up for another promotion," Mom boasted.

"Good for him, he deserves it." Jesse forced enthusiasm into his voice. Somehow, it was always okay when Randy missed family functions because of work. It was never okay when Jesse had to skip one because he was at the firehouse.

"Someday, that brother of yours is going to rule the world." Dad had said it a million times, but it never got easier to swallow. Every step Randy took up the ladder seemed to push Jesse farther down it from Dad's point of view. While Dad never came out and said it, it was clear Jesse's father felt that a man who worked with his hands only did so because his brain wasn't up to higher tasks.

"I don't doubt it, Dad," Jesse admitted wearily. "I'll just settle for being King of the Grill."

Mom looked eagerly at the petite fillet he'd marinated just the way she liked it. "That is just fine by me. Jesse, honey, this smells fantastic. You will make some lucky lady very happy one of these days." Her eyes held just a tint of sadness, reminding Jesse that the ink was barely dry on Randy's divorce papers. His brother's raging career successes had inflicted a few casualties of late, and Mom had been disappointed to watch her grandma prospects walk out the door behind Randy's neglected wife. This past winter had been hard on the Sykes family, that was for sure. Was Dad clueless to all those wounds? Or did he just choose to ignore what he couldn't solve?

They were in love…once…his mom and dad. Now they just sort of existed in the same life, side by side but not close. Randy had married because he was "supposed to." As if he needed to check off some box in his life plan. Jesse didn't want to just make some appropriate lady "very happy." When he fell, it would be deep and strong and he would sweep that love of his life clean off her feet.

It just wasn't looking as though that would be anytime soon.

Chapter Two

"Done." Charlotte Taylor finished signing her name at the bottom of the long sales document. She put her pen—the beautiful new fountain pen she'd bought especially for this occasion—down on the conference table as if she were planting a flag. She was, in a way. The knot in her stomach already knew this was a big deal. A good big deal. The way to get her life back on track and prove Monarch was only a bump in the road, not the end of the line. She looked up and gave her companions a victorious smile. "The cottage is officially mine."

"I still can't believe you're going through with this." Charlotte's best friend, Melba, sat with her baby on her lap, trying to look supportive but appearing more worried than pleased. "I mean, I'm happy for you and all, but you're sure?"

Charlotte had done nothing but mull the matter over in the week since the layoff, and while the timing might look wrong on the outside, she'd come to the conclusion that it was actually perfect. She needed this, needed a project to balance the stress of a job search. When she'd gone to see the cottage again and the seller had been willing to knock down the price for a cash offer, Charlotte felt as if Mima was showing her it was time to act. "I am. If I do it now, I'll have the time to do it right. And you know me—I'll have a new job before long. This is exactly the kind of thing Mima would have wanted me to do with my inheritance."

"It's nice to see someone your age so excited to put down roots." The broker—a plump, older woman named Helen Bearson, who looked more suited to baking pies than hawking vacation properties—smiled back as she handed Charlotte the keys. The large, old keys tumbled heavy and serious into Charlotte's hand. "I'm sure you'll be very happy after the renovations. Gordon Falls is a lovely place to get away to—but you already knew that."

Melba gently poked the baby Maria's sweet button nose and cooed, "Aunt Charlotte always did know exactly what she wanted, Maria. Now you'll get to see her much more often."

Charlotte couldn't really fault Melba's singsong, oh-so-sweet voice; new moms were supposed to adore their babies like that. It was charming. She'd probably be even more sugary when her time as a new mom came—if it ever came—and Maria was adorable. She'd been baby-perfect, happy and quiet for the entire long real estate transaction, and Charlotte had been grateful for the company at such an important event, even if it did take over an hour. Charlotte herself felt as if her hand would never uncramp from signing her name so many times.

Funny how even happy milestones could be so exhausting. Squeezing the new keys tight—well, new to her at least, for they looked giant and cumbersome next to her slick apartment and car keys—she exhaled. This wasn't an indulgence; this was a lifeline. Just for fun, Charlotte rattled the keys playfully over the baby's head. Maria's little gray eyes lit up at the tinkling sound, her chubby hands reaching up in a way that had all three women saying "Aww."

Awe, actually. She'd done it. The keys she held belonged to a cottage Charlotte now owned. It was an exhilarating, thrilling kind of fear, this huge leap. The cottage had become a tangible promise to herself, a symbol that future success was still ahead of her and she could still be in command of the blessings God had given her. No matter what her new job would be, no matter where her rented city apartment might shift, this cottage would be the fixed point, the home ready to welcome her on weekends and vacations. She'd boasted of feeling established in her job at Monarch, but the truth was today was what really made her feel like an adult. She'd never owned anything more permanent than a car before this. Her chest pinched in a happy, frantic kind of excitement.

"Thanks, Mima." She liked to think Mima was as pleased as she was, sending down her blessing from heaven as surely as if a rainbow appeared in the bank conference room. Once she'd prayed and made the decision, it felt as if Mima had orchestrated the whole thing—in cahoots with God to line the details up so perfectly that the purchase had been swift and nearly effortless. Yes, she was in command of the blessings God had given her—and that was what she'd sought: a firm defense against the uncertainties of a woman "between jobs."

Sure, Melba had made the same noise about practicality that Mom had made. Charlotte knew it might have been more sensible to buy a Chicago apartment and stay in the area to job-hunt, but Mima hadn't left her the money to be sensible. Mima was all about leaps of the heart, and right now Charlotte didn't know where her next job would take her, but she knew her heart kept pulling her toward Gordon Falls as her spot to get away. She'd spent so many weekends here, the guest bed at Melba's house had a Charlotte-shaped dent in it. The hustle and sparkle of Chicago would always be wonderful, but Mima's bequest meant she could own this cottage and rent a nice place in Chicago near her next job for the weekdays. That felt like a smart plan, and everyone knew smart wasn't always practical. Who knew? The way telecommuting was taking off these days, she might work full-time out of Gordon Falls someday in the future.

"Congratulations," Melba said, trying again to be supportive.

Poor Melba. She'd always be too cautious to ever launch an adventure like this. Melba had too many people needing her—a husband, until recently her late father, and now Maria—to ever throw caution to the wind. Charlotte would have to show her how exhilarating it could be. "I own a cottage. I'm landed gentry."

Melba winced as she untangled a lock of her hair from Maria's exploring fingers. "That might be overstating things, but I am glad you'll be here. Gordon Falls could use a few more of us young whippersnappers."

"I couldn't agree more," Mrs. Bearson confirmed as she slid the files into the needlepoint tote bag that served as her briefcase. "I'm delighted to see so many of you younger people coming into town and settling down."

Settling down. The words fit, but the sensation was just the opposite; more of a leaping forward. It was the most alive she'd felt since that harrowing exit from the Monarch offices. Renovating this cottage was going to be about doing life on purpose instead of having it done to you by accident. Today declared Charlotte her own person, with her own roots to plant.

The older woman extended a hand. "Welcome to Gordon Falls, Charlotte Taylor. You'll love it here."

Charlotte shook her hand. "I know I will. Thanks for everything."

"My pleasure. Tootle-loo!" With a waggle of her fingers, she bustled from the conference room to the bank's lobby, where she headed over to say hello to several people.

Melba caught Charlotte's eye. "Tootle-loo?"

Charlotte winced. "She's said that every time we've met. Odd, but cute." She stared at the keys in her hand, cool at first but now warm and friendly to her touch. "I own a cottage."

"You do."

She'd been there three times in the past two days, but the need to see it again, to turn the key in the lock with her own hand as the owner, pressed against her heart. "Let's go see my cottage. My cottage. I want to make myself a cup of tea in my cottage. I brought some tea leaves and a kettle with me and everything."

Baby Maria's response to the invitation was to scrunch up her face and erupt in a tiny little rage. She'd been darling up until now, but it was clear that her patience was coming to an end. "I think Miss Maria needs to nurse and to nap. Much as I'd like to be there, I think we had better head home." Melba put a hand on Charlotte's arm. "Will you be okay on your own?"

"Just fine." That was the whole point of the cottage, wasn't it? When she thought about it, it was fitting that the first hours Charlotte spent in the cottage as its owner were on her own. "I'll be back for dinner, okay?" The cottage wasn't in any shape to call home just yet, so she'd opted to stay a few days at Melba's while she got things set up right.

"See you later, Miss Taylor of the landed gentry," Melba called above Maria's escalating cries. "Enjoy your new castle."

Jesse wrenched open another of the cottage's stuck windows and waved the smoke away from his face. The air was as sour as his stomach. He could barely believe he was standing in his cottage—only it wasn't his anymore now—talking to the new owner. Talk about a kick to the gut. "Exactly when did the stove catch on fire?"

The panicked blonde next to him pushed a lock of hair back off her forehead. "About five minutes after I turned it on." She pointed to a charred kettle now hissing steam in the stained porcelain sink. "Tea. I was just trying to make tea." Her eyes wandered to the fire truck now idling in her driveway, dwarfing her tiny blue hatchback. "I'm sorry. I probably overreacted by calling you all in for such a little fire. I was too panicked to think straight. I just bought the place today and I didn't know what else to do."

She was so apologetic and rattled, it was hard to stay annoyed at her. People were always apologizing for calling the fire department. Jesse never got that. It's not like anyone ever apologized for seeing their doctor or calling a plumber. She had no reason to be upset for calling the fire department, even for a little fire. Kitchen fires could be dangerous. One look at the dilapidated 1960s electric range told him any number of problems could have escalated from an open flame there. Sure it was a quaint-looking appliance, but he of all people knew suppliers who made stoves with just as much of that trendy vintage charm but with modern safety features. "Even a small fire isn't anything to mess with. Small fires can get very big very fast."

Of course, if *he* had been the new owner, he'd have had the sense to make sure the stove was safe before turning it on and starting the fire in the first place. The sting of his current situation surged up again. Why did he have to be on duty when this particular call came in? Why did he have to find out the cottage he'd intended to buy had been sold this way? He picked up his helmet from the chipped Formica counter, forcing kindness into his tone. "Look, don't be worried. You did the right thing, Ms...."

"Taylor. Charlotte Taylor." So that was the name of his pretty little adversary.

"Don't ever hesitate to call on us, Charlotte. Especially if you're on your own. It's why we're here, okay?"

Her eyes scanned the smoke still hovering close to the kitchen's tin ceiling. Jesse had always thought the ceiling was this kitchen's best feature. Stuff like that was hard to find these days. Would she appreciate that or tear it down and put in a boring ceiling with sterile track lighting? "Okay." She mostly mumbled the word, her face pale and drawn tight.

She didn't look anything close to okay. Her nerves were so obviously jangled they practically echoed around the empty kitchen. "If you don't mind me asking... why the sudden need for tea? You're not even moved in, from the looks of it." Her reply might let him know what her plans were for the place. If she was plotting a teardown and wasn't planning to move in at all, he could skip the preliminaries and get right down to hating her this minute.

She flushed. "It was a celebration thing. I just signed

the papers on the place today. I told Melba I just wanted to have a cup of tea on my new deck."

How had he missed this? The facts wove together in his brain, making everything worse. "You're Melba's friend?"

Chief Bradens had mentioned his wife's friend was buying a weekend cottage in town. Never in a million years did Jesse consider it might be *this* cottage. Now, annoyed as he was, he'd have to be nice. A friend of the fire chief's wife demanded special care. "No harm done that I can see." He put his helmet back down on the counter as he swallowed his sore pride. "I should check the rest of the place. Just to be safe," he said over his shoulder as he began banging open the two remaining kitchen windows when they refused to budge.

She shrugged. "Probably a good idea."

He knew the rooms of this house. A visual inspection wasn't really necessary, but it might give him a last look at the place before she stripped it of all its charm. Charlotte followed him around the empty rooms while he peered at light switches, tested the knobs on heating registers and tried the fuses in the antiquated fuse box. Did she know what she was getting into here? This was no starter project for a hobby house flipper. "You can still keep lots of the place's charm, but you're gonna need some serious updating." He raised his eyebrows at her resulting frown. "You knew that going in, didn't you?"

"I did."

She did not. Now that was just dirty pool, letting someone like her beat him to a place like this.

Some jilted part of him wanted to tell her the house was chock-full of danger, but it wasn't true. Nothing looked dangerous to his contractor's eye, just old and likely finicky. The greatest danger she faced was blowing a fuse if she plugged her hair dryer in while the dishwasher was running. Charlotte had nice hair. Platinum blond in a city-sleek rather than elegant cut. She looked relatively smart, but what did he know? Do smart people set their teakettles on fire?

He avoided looking at her by inspecting the stove knobs. "Nothing about wiring came up in the home inspection?" He almost hated to add, "You did *have* a home inspection, didn't you?" It was killing him—she looked as if she didn't even own a hammer, much less the belt sander it would take to bring those hardwood floors in the dining room up to snuff. Still, she had a certain spunk about her. It hadn't been there when he and the other guys first barged in the door, but he could see it now returning to her eyes. If she made the right choices, she might do okay. Not that he wanted her to succeed.

"Of course I did. Only now I'm thinking maybe it wasn't so thorough." She crossed her arms over her chest and her eyebrows furrowed together. "Honestly, the guy looked like he did inspections for laughs in between fishing trips. Mrs. Bearson said he was reliable, but…"

Helen Bearson. He could have guessed she'd made the sale. Helen was a sweet lady, but the kind Jesse referred to as a "hobby broker." Dollars to donuts the inspector was her brother. "Larry Barker?" Even someone he resented as much as Charlotte Taylor deserved better than that guy—Jesse wouldn't pay him to inspect a shoe box.

Charlotte raised an eyebrow. "A mistake, huh?"

He couldn't just sit there and let her make choices from what was likely bad information. Well, he *could,* but he wasn't the kind of guy who would—even under these circumstances. Jesse shucked off his heavy firefighter's coat and squatted down in front of the appliance, opening the oven door and peering inside. "Let's just say he wouldn't be my first choice," he said, giving Barker more benefit of the doubt than he deserved. "I haven't seen anything that should have stopped your sale." In fact, he knew there were no massive problems because he'd given the house a thorough once-over himself, far beyond his ten-minute walkthrough just now. Still, the word *sale* stuck in his throat. "This could really be just an old stove, not faulty wiring or anything." He stared at a layer of grime so thick he could sign his name in it with a fingernail. "I don't think this has been used in a couple of years. You'll want to replace it."

She groaned. "But I love the way this one looks. Does it cost a fortune to rehab a stove?"

Dark brown eyes and blond hair—the effect was striking, even with a frown on her face. "You can't really rehab a stove. Still there are ones that look old-fashioned but function like new. They're pricey, but you had to have known you were going to put some money into the place."

"Well of course I did, but I was hoping to wait longer than two hours before the first repair."

Despite his irritation, Jesse liked her sense of humor. He glanced out the window to where the three other firemen were putting gear back into the truck. Normally he didn't fish for contractor work while on firefighting duty—especially given this particular circumstance—but she was pretty and clearly on her own and, well, seemed at a loss. Sure he'd regret it but unable to stop himself, Jesse swallowed the last of his pride and pulled a business card from his pants pocket. "I'm a licensed contractor over at Mondale Construction. If you like, give me a call tomorrow and I'll walk through the house with you over the weekend. I can go over what Larry said and either confirm it or tell you differently. I'll help you figure out what really needs work right away and what can wait until you've gotten over the sticker shock." If he couldn't have the house, maybe he could at least get the work, much as it would dent his ego.

She narrowed her eyes. "Why would you do that?"

He hated when people gave him "the contractor out to take you to the cleaners" look. "Because you're a friend of the chief's. Because I'm a nice guy." *Because I'm an idiot and am trying not to be a sore loser.* "And because I can make sure Mondale gives you a good price for work I could do and recommend a couple of guys for the other stuff—guys who will do it right and not empty your checkbook for the sport of it."

She took the card but still eyed him. Good. She shouldn't be trusting everyone who walked in here offering to help her, even him. She looked smarter than that, and he could bring himself to be glad she was acting like it. "So maybe you really are a nice guy," she said, still sounding a bit doubtful.

"Don't take my word for it. Look, you ought to know I don't normally pitch work on duty. Only I think Chief and Melba might ride me if I didn't offer my help, given the—" he waved at the smoke now almost completely gone from the kitchen "—circumstances. It's the least I can do."

She looked unconvinced, and a part of him was ready to be rid of the obligation. He'd tried, wasn't that enough? He gave it one last shot of total honesty. "Frankly, this place is a contractor's dream—good bones but needing loads of work. And I could use the work." After a second, he looked out the window and added, "Why don't you think about it? I've got to get back to the truck anyway—the guys are waiting for me."

She planted her hands on her hips. "No, I don't need to think about it. Can you come by after church Sunday?"

She went to church. Of course she went to church; she was a friend of Chief Bradens and his wife. Not wanting to look like the stranger to services that he was, he hazarded a guess based on when he usually saw his friends out and about on Sundays. "Eleven-thirty?"

"Perfect." She smiled—an "I'm rattled but I'll make it" lopsided grin that told him she'd do okay even if this wasn't the last disaster of her new home. Her new home. Life was cruel some days.

Jesse nodded at the kitchen's vintage molding and bay widows. "This will make a nice weekend place. You'll do just fine."

She made a face. "That's just what I was telling myself when the stove caught on fire."

"Everything looks okay, but I'd hold off on teatime until we check out all the appliances if I were you." His radio beeped, letting him know the rest of the crew outside was getting impatient. "Once you get the rest of your utilities up and running, turn on the fridge so we can check how cold it gets."

She perked up. "Did that already. Turned it on, I mean." To prove her point, she opened the ancient-looking refrigerator and made a show of peering inside. "Chilling down, nothing scary inside." Her head popped back out and she shut the door. "The dishwasher, I'm not so sure. It looks older than I am."

For an intriguing second, Jesse wondered just how old that was. She looked about his age, but he'd never been good at guessing those things. "Yeah, I'd hold off." He gestured to the single mug sitting beside a box of fancy-looking tea on the otherwise bare 1950s-era Formica countertop. "Not like you've got a load of dishes to do anyhow."

That lit a spark in her eyes. "Oh, I own tons of dishes. I collect vintage china. I've got enough to fill all the shelves in this house and my apartment back in Chicago twice over. Not that I'd put any of them in this old dinosaur, anyway." She shrugged. "Well, thanks, Officer—" she squinted down at the card "—Sykes." She held out her hand.

He shook it. "I'm not an officer, I'm just part of the volunteer brigade. So Jesse will do. I'll see you Sunday at eleven-thirty. And as for your new house celebration, go on down to Karl's Koffee and tell him what happened. If I know Karl, he'll give you a free cup of tea and maybe some pie to smooth things over. You deserve a better welcome to Gordon Falls than one from us." Jesse decided he'd call from the truck and ask Karl to do just that. Only, knowing Karl, he'd have done it with no nudging at all.

He felt a tiny bit better for pulling that sweet smile from her. "Maybe I'll do just that. Thanks."

Jesse tried to ignore the teasing looks that greeted him as he climbed into the truck. "Isn't she the prettiest run of the day." Yorky, an older member of the department who could never be counted on for subtlety, bumped Jesse on the shoulder.

"Of the week," Wally Forman corrected, waggling an eyebrow for emphasis. "Only it's not so fun for you given the circumstances, is it, Jesse?"

"Could have fooled me," Yorky snickered.

Jesse merely grunted and settled farther down in his seat. Maybe Wally would let it go.

Wally stared at him. "It is, isn't it? That's the one?"

Narrowing his eyes in the strongest "not now" glare he could manage, Jesse didn't answer.

Wally leaned back in his seat and pointed at Jesse. "It is. I knew it. Oh, man, tough break."

Yorky looked at Jesse, then at Wally, then back at Jesse again. "What? What am I missing?"

Jesse cocked his head to one side in an "I'm warning you" scowl aimed straight at Wally.

Not that it did any good. "That's the house. The one Jesse talked about buying. Sweetie-Pie up there just bought it right out from underneath him. How many more months before you would have saved up enough for the down payment, Sykes? It had to be soon."

Was Wally going out of his way to drive the sore point home? "Two." Up until this moment Jesse had managed to let Little Miss China Cabinet's sweet smile tamp down his irritation at being beat to the purchase table.

Yorky hissed. "Ouch!"

"Yeah," Jesse repeated, craning his neck back to look at the tidy little cottage. "Ouch."

Chapter Three

"Melba, I'm not the first person in the world to lose my job," Charlotte told her dear friend as they sat at her table after dinner that night. Charlotte had managed to avoid the topic of conversation with Melba for days, but tonight Clark was down at the firehouse for the evening and her friend had cornered her in the kitchen. "I wasn't even the last at Monarch—there were three other envelopes on Alice's desk."

Melba had Maria settled in the crook of her arm. "I'm just worried about you. Are you okay? You seem to be taking it well, but…"

Charlotte kept telling herself that she was handling it as well as could be expected, but she also spent too many moments stuffing down a deep panic. "Do I have a choice?"

"Not you. You'd never go to pieces, even at something like this." She caught Charlotte's eye. "But you could. I mean, don't feel like you have to put on any kind of front with me. I've gone to pieces enough times in front of you."

While Charlotte was sure Melba meant what she said, the idea of giving in to the fear—even for a moment and even with a dear friend—felt like opening the big green floodgates at the end of town. Best to keep that door firmly shut. "I'm okay. I think I'm okay. I mean, I'm scared—you're supposed to be in my situation—but I can push through this. I'm choosing to feel more like I'm waiting for whatever God's got around the corner than I've been broadsided by a job change."

Melba leaned in. "The best part is you get to wait here. I'll be so happy to have you around."

"Well, part of the time. I expect I'll need to take lots of trips back to Chicago for job-search stuff and interviews eventually. Only it'll be great to have the cottage as a distraction. All the books say to take on inspiring new projects so it doesn't become all about the job search. This is a great time to get a serious creative groove on. I need a place outside of my résumé to channel all this energy."

All that was true, but there was still a small corner of her chest that felt as if she had planted her flag at the top of a very high mountain with no idea how to climb back down. She nodded to the thick file of plans, the one she'd taken from her desk on her last day at Monarch. "I wonder if Mima had any idea the incredible gift this is going to be. To get to fix this place up exactly the way I want it? To have enough to do that after I bought it? Debt free? It's a huge blessing."

Melba gave her a cautious smile. "I know you got it at a great price, but it needs so much work." She thumbed through the file of clippings and swatches with her free hand while Maria gave a tiny sigh of baby contentment in her other arm. "Don't you think it's a big risk to take at a time like this?"

Charlotte shrugged. "Yes, it is a big risk. But it's a worthwhile risk. Just the thought of being able to do this up right gives me so much energy. I don't care if I have to buy shelving instead of shoes. Or stop eating until October."

"You're not going to fix up the whole place and decorate it all at once, are you?" Melba turned to a magazine page showing chintz kitchen curtains. "Won't that cost more than you have?"

"I *have* to do some of the fixing up as soon as possible. The stove, the heating, the upstairs bathroom—they need renovation before they'll be usable, and all that stuff has to be done if I'm going to be able to live there. Do I need the designer concrete sink right away? Well, I don't know yet. It's probably smarter to get exactly what I want now—once you start ripping stuff out, you might as well do it right the first time rather than rip stuff up again a year later."

"Charlotte…"

"I know, I know. Stop worrying—I'm not going to take my aggressions out at the home decorating store. I should probably have the home improvement channels blocked off my cable service for now. But since I don't have a job, I can't even afford cable television, so that solves that anyway, doesn't it?" She leaned back in her chair, as if the sheer weight of Melba's doubts had pushed her there. "This is going to be fine. Really. I won't let this get out of hand."

Melba pushed the file back across the table to Charlotte. "Easy to say now, but these things have a way of snowballing. Even the remodeling costs for the house I inherited from Dad sent Clark and me reeling."

When Melba's father had died last year after a long battle with Alzheimer's, it left Clark and Melba to remake her childhood home into the one that now housed her new family. The transition had been complicated and expensive—going beyond what it would have cost in both time and money to start fresh with a new house—but it just proved Charlotte's point: the house gave off a palpable sense of history. She'd felt something like it from the cottage that first visit. The once-charming cottage seemed to beckon to her, begging to be restored. She knew it was a risky prospect, but she couldn't make herself feel as if she'd made the wrong choice. She'd chosen a challenging path, yes, but not a wrong one. "I'm going to be fine, Melba. Now let's drop the subject and let me hold that baby."

Melba stood up and handed Maria to Charlotte. As Maria snuggled in against her shoulder, Charlotte breathed in the darling scent of baby-girl curls. "You've got the best of both worlds, Maria. Your mama's curls and your daddy's red hair. You may hate it when you're five, but guys are gonna follow you like ducklings when you're seventeen."

Melba laughed as she warmed Charlotte's tea and set down a plate of cookies. "Clark's already informed me Maria will be banned from dating until she's thirty. And no firefighters."

Charlotte applied an expression of false shock. "Well, I'll back him up on the 'no firefighters' policy, but that's kind of a tough sell. He's the fire chief, isn't he?"

Sitting back down, Melba laughed again. "I think it's *because* he's chief. He's seen a little too much of the department's social life or heard a little too much in the locker room."

"They don't seem that rough around the edges to me. As a matter of fact, Jesse Sykes seems like a stand-up guy." Charlotte could feel Maria softening against her shoulder. Melba was right—the world was always a better place with a baby drooling on your shoulder.

"He's an original, that's for sure." Melba selected a cookie and dunked it in her tea. "I don't know about stand-up, but he sure stands out. You can trust him, though. He did some of the work here on the house. Good work, if you don't mind the singing."

"The what?"

"Jesse has a habit of breaking out in Motown hits. If you haven't heard him yet, you will. Don't you remember he sang at Alex and JJ's wedding?"

"*That* was Jesse Sykes?" Charlotte recalled a rather impressive version of "My Girl" at her cousin's wedding. She tried to imagine Jesse's soulful voice echoing in the cottage living room, but she couldn't conjure up the image. "Mostly he just made wisecracks when I talked to him this time. Funny guy."

"Oh, he's a cutup, that's for sure. And a good firefighter. Clark wouldn't put up with his antics otherwise." Melba got a conniving look on her face. "You should hire him. I think he'd be good for you. An upbeat guy to have around in a tight spot."

Charlotte narrowed her eyes. "Oh, no, you don't."

"Don't what?" Melba's innocent blink hid nothing.

Charlotte whispered into Maria's ear, "Your mama's getting ideas."

"I am not."

"Oh, yes, you are. I know you too well. Look, I know we were discussing behavior, not profession, but he's a fireman, Melba. I won't get into a relationship with a first responder no matter how well behaved. We've been through this how many times? Nothing's changed. I've got way too many memories of sitting up nights with Mom at the kitchen table."

"Your dad was a policeman, I know, but—"

"But nothing. Same stress, different uniform. Melba,

I've got nothing against you and Clark, and goodness knows JJ's done terrific at the firehouse, but I know what I can handle and what I can't. I've never dated someone who does that kind of work and I don't plan to start now."

A tiny war was going on in Jesse's chest—and in his pride—as he walked up the overgrown sidewalk to Charlotte's cottage Sunday morning. This was supposed to be his cottage. The place needed loads of work, and he knew he was the best man to complete it. He'd planned the rehab of this place a dozen times, imagining living in the home as he upgraded fixtures, appliances and wiring until he could turn around and sell it for a tidy profit. Or even stay there and use it as the showcase for what he could do with other properties. But that opportunity was lost now.

The only opportunity left in this situation was to be the guy hired for the renovation job. If a woman could afford a vacation cottage at Charlotte's age, she probably wouldn't haggle over the cost the place would require to be done up right. His business sense knew that made her an excellent customer even if she was a thorn in his side. The house needed loads of work, and loads of work could mean a big check for Mondale and for him. As he lay in bed last night, Jesse told himself a job this size could leave him with even more funds than he'd anticipated making over the summer. Funds to buy another house—bigger and better to soothe his wounded pride and show his father just how savvy a businessman he could be.

All this should have had him dreaming up the perfect sales pitch as he approached the door—and yet for some reason, he wasn't. He prided himself on knowing how to optimize a customer with deep pockets, only Charlotte Taylor didn't have that entitled look about her. In fact, she looked a little…lost. The way he'd looked when he'd first put on the bulky, cumbersome firefighter's gear—right at the launch of a dream, forcing an outer confidence that didn't quite cover the dazzled and doubtful person on the inside.

As he pushed the rusty doorbell button, Jesse still wasn't sure how he was going to play it for this meeting. *Just wing it,* he told himself. *You wing it all the time.* He pushed the button again, listening for the chimes inside the house once he noticed the living room window was open to his left.

No sound. Sometimes it was useful to start a customer off with a small project, but he'd planned on something larger than a broken doorbell. He knocked on the door loudly and leaned over the wrought-iron railing to yell into the window. "Charlotte!"

A second knock and another yell produced no reply. He pivoted to see her little blue car wasn't in the cottage drive. Maybe church ran long today. He could just start without her while he waited. After checking his watch, Jesse pulled out his notes.

He'd already made his own list of what the house needed, but he'd go through the process of re-creating a list to suit her taste. He just hoped it wouldn't clash with the character of the house he saw so clearly. Catering to a client's whims was one thing—ignoring his own clear ideas on this particular place was going to be quite another. Still, he'd do it to rack up enough funds to move forward. He was bone-tired of delays and detours, not to mention his father's ever-increasing digs.

Pacing the cottage's front stoop, he toed boards and pushed harder on the railing only to have it creak and pull out from its mountings. He added the doorbell and railing to his handwritten list and began scanning the front of the house for anything he'd missed.

He'd added four more items by the time Charlotte's small blue hatchback pulled into the drive behind his large brown pickup.

"Sorry!" she called, breathless and airy in a blue print dress with a lacy sweater that rippled behind her as she came up the steps. "Church went on forever. I mean, a good forever, but enough to make me late. I hope you weren't waiting long."

Jesse waited for her to say something like "I noticed you weren't in church." Or "Have you ever gone?" or the half dozen other thinly disguised recommendations he got from Melba, Clark and various other friends around town. "No, I'm fine. Hey, JJ told me you're her cousin. You were at the wedding, too, weren't you? On the boat?"

"Wedding of the year, wasn't it?"

As the only female firefighter in Gordon Falls, JJ Cushman stuck out already before her legendary wedding to Alex Cushman on a steamboat on the Gordon River. "A big shindig, that's for sure."

"And then there's my other cousin, JJ's brother, Max." She fished for her keys and wrestled the old door lock open. "And Melba's baby is my new goddaughter. I know lots of people in Gordon Falls."

They walked through the front hallway to the kitchen, where she plunked an enormous tapestry handbag—a vintage artsy-looking thing, he was glad to notice— down on the kitchen counter. "And now I know Karl. You were right. He did give me a slice of pie for my troubles." She sighed, a happy, shoulder-heaving, contented sigh. "This is a nice town."

It was, most of the time. "It has its moments."

Charlotte began digging through the massive bag. "I made a list last night of the things I think the house needs—as a jumping-off point." She pulled out a notebook with Victorian ladies dancing on the cover. "I'm no expert, though."

Jesse put a hand to his chest. "That's okay, because I am. Only there's an awkward question I really should ask first."

"Where do I want to hide the bodies?" She didn't need the pink lipstick to show off that dynamic smile; her eyes lit up with humor.

The joke made the next question easier to ask. "No, what's your budget?"

"Oh, that." He couldn't quite gauge her response.

"I mean, you don't have to tell me," he backpedaled, suddenly feeling his poor-loser wounds had run off with his diplomacy, "but it's better if I know. I can make smarter recommendations if I have a total-figure picture on the whole project."

Charlotte hoisted herself up to sit on the vacant countertop. "That's the best part—I don't have a budget. My grandma left me enough money to do this—at least I'm pretty certain she did. This place was a leap of faith." She didn't come out and say "unlimited funds," but her eyes sure looked as though she was ready to spend. *Must be nice to have that kind of cash.* Jesse ignored the sharp curl of envy wrapped around his gut.

Instead, he focused on how she fit in the house. Houses—even half-built or long since run-down houses—always had personalities to him. He'd sensed this cottage's personality way back, and looking at her perched on the counter, he knew her personality absolutely suited the vibe of this place. Had he just finished the remodeling, he'd probably have been delighted to sell it to her. He just couldn't get there quite yet—for all her charm, Charlotte Taylor was still the agent of the delay in his achieving his dreams.

She looked around the room with wistful eyes. "Mima was amazing." The grief was still fresh, glistening in her eyes and present in the catch of her words. Whoever this grandmother was, Charlotte missed her very much.

"Did Mima leave you her china?" Jesse wasn't quite sure what made him ask.

Her eyes went wide; big velvet-brown pools of curiosity. "How did you know?"

"You said you collect." Jesse began working his way around the kitchen, pulling drawers open, checking cabinet hinges, forcing himself to see the house through her eyes than through his own loss. "It seemed a natural guess that she'd leave you hers if you were that close."

"We were." Charlotte's voice was thick with memory. "Mima was the most astounding woman. She didn't have an easy life, but she got so much out of every moment, you know?" For a second Jesse worried Charlotte was going to break into tears right there on the countertop, but she just took a deep breath and tucked her hands under her knees. "She'd love this place."

Needing to lighten the moment, Jesse raised the charred teakettle from its place in the sink. "Even the smoke-signal tea service?"

Charlotte laughed. She had a great laugh—lively and full and light. "She might have liked the drama, but Mima was a coffee drinker. 'Strong as love and black as night,' she used to say. Drank four cups a day right up until the end, even when her doctors yelled at her."

It would be so much easier to begrudge Charlotte

the sale if she weren't so…sweet. Sweet? That wasn't usually the kind of word he'd use to describe a woman, but it was the one that kept coming to mind with her. Only, she was more than sweet. She had an edge about her. An energy. She was probably more like her Mima than she knew. Spunky, maybe? No, that sounded ridiculous. Vivacious—that was it.

Jesse dragged his mind back to the task at hand. "Let's walk through the house and identify what needs doing."

It didn't take long. Half the needed improvements had already been in his head, and the other half came cascading down upon him as he assumed his contractor's mind-set and considered the house with her needs in mind. Every time the bitter thought of what he would have wanted threatened to overtake him, he wrote down a dollar figure next to a project to show himself what Charlotte's business could mean for his future. By the time he left, Jesse was looking at a proposal that might get him down payments on two different investment properties, and she didn't seem too fazed by it. Things were looking up.

Chapter Four

Jesse watched Charlotte reading through his written proposal on her back porch the next afternoon. Despite how easy it was to chat with her—and how unfairly easy she was to like—the entire situation still hung off-kilter and uncomfortable inside him like a bad joke. He admired her enthusiasm, but it felt like a punch to his ribs at the same time. Had he shown that kind of energy, the singular focus she now displayed toward this house, he'd already own the cottage by now.

Even though she'd been in town only a few days, he'd heard from several people—Chief Bradens, Melba, his fellow firefighter JJ, even JJ's brother, Max—about how Charlotte had gushed over her affection for the cottage. For crying out loud, it seemed even Karl at the coffee shop had gotten a speech about what she planned to do with the place. She'd spout off her plans to anyone who would listen.

Had he shown her initiative, acting more aggressively, more single-mindedly on his plans—the way Randy always acted when it came to business deals—Helen Bearson might have tipped him off that someone else had shown interest in the property. He could have found a way to inch past those final two months and purchase the property now. But no, his claim never went further than a comment to his folks or a vague remark to the other guys on the truck when they went past the vacant house. He'd never done anything more than occasional blue-sky thinking aloud. The plans had been there: real and detailed, meticulously compiled. But he'd kept them to himself, not wanting to be made the butt of more jokes or criticism if things didn't work out. Now the spreadsheet calculating his accrued savings toward the goal felt like a misfire. No, worse: a dud.

Of course, Jesse knew better. His nobler side told him he had no right to his resentment. He had no practical claim to the cottage. This was just another example of his biggest flaw: always hatching plans and spending too long perfecting them to get around to acting on them. Dad would probably be gratified that his trademark inaction had once again come back to bite him. He'd lost the cottage, fair and square. *You snooze, you lose. You've always known that. Maybe now you know it for real.*

The only consolation—and it was slim consolation at that—was how Jesse's gut still told him she belonged in that house. She had on these old-fashioned-looking shoes that would have looked ridiculous on anyone else, but with her flowing pastel dress and the fluttery scarf she wore, she looked as though she belonged right there on the cottage steps. "Vintage chic," his mom would probably call it. All soft and frilly around the edges but definitely not stodgy, and with an artsy edge that let him know she'd have great taste. She wouldn't gut the place and modernize it, stripping away all the history and charm—she'd do it right.

She flipped over the final page of the document he'd

given her. "Wow, it's a lot, isn't it?" Despite her bright optimism, he could still read hints of sadness and confusion in her eyes. Trouble was, that determination just made him like her more. This job was starting to feel as though it could become a tangled mess all too easily—and even a mess-up like him knew it was never smart to mix business with pleasure. Even when the pleasure could land him a fat paycheck.

"It's a big job, yes. The results will be fantastic, though. You'd double your money if you ever sold."

"I won't sell." No buyer's remorse from this buyer, that was certain. He got the feeling that once Charlotte Taylor set her course, she was unstoppable.

"Okay, so you want to stay. Well, we know there are some basic repairs you'll need no matter what—like the stove and the upstairs bathroom—even if you do change your mind and decide to sell…."

"Which I won't."

"Which you won't," he echoed. "We can start with those and schedule out the cosmetic fixes and upgrades later. That way you start basic, but keep your options wide open."

She leaned back against the porch stair railing. At least this railing held, not like the wobbly one at her front door. Jesse grimaced as he remembered the photo of the gorgeous wrought-iron railing sitting in his file back home. "Maybe, but first on the list has to be my new claw-footed bathtub."

She'd gushed over the style of the old tub in the upstairs bathroom, saying she'd picked out some new-fangled Jacuzzi version that still looked antique. "New is great, but you could also repair the one you already have. Old fixtures like that are hard to find and worth keeping—especially if you want to go the sensible route."

Her eyes flashed at the mention of *sensible,* and she straightened her back with an air of defiance. "Or maybe I don't compromise. Maybe I use all this free time to do the renovation *exactly* the way I want while I can."

"Free time?" Jesse couldn't help asking.

"I'm between jobs at the moment." There was a flash of hurt in her eyes as she said the words, but it faded quickly. "It's just a temporary situation. It's not like I won't find a new job. I'm very good at what I do. Lots of companies are ramping up their online commerce. Textile arts are big business these days, you know."

She didn't strike Jesse as the sensible type. More the artistic, impulsive type. Those customers were always the most fun—provided they had pockets as deep as their imaginations—which maybe still applied to Charlotte Taylor. He didn't really know many details about what her financial situation was, nor was it his place to ask. Still, he'd seen this before, watching a customer compensate for some loss in their life by going overboard on a build. A guy's divorce-driven five-car garage had bought Jesse his new truck. After all, a smart businessman gives the customer what they want, not necessarily what they need. "You could do that."

"I could do that." Her face took on the most amazing energy when she got an idea. She was going to be a fun client to work with, and certainly easy on the eyes.

Jesse suddenly found himself wondering if he could walk the line on this. Could he encourage her, suggest the smartest choices for what she wanted? Could he balance the indulgence of her whims while warning her against something that would prove to be a foolish purchase? Viewed practically, her windfall of free time might allow him to get more work done in less time.

He nodded to the proposal. "I'm not saying you have to compromise. A job this big would be hard to do while you were working full-time. If you set your mind to it, we could be done by September. If you've got the cash now, the timing might be perfect."

She pointed at him, jangling the slew of silver bangles on her wrist. "Exactly how I see it. God's never late and He's never early."

"Huh?"

"Something Mima always said. About God's timing always being perfect, just like you mentioned. And I've always taken Mima's advice."

"You don't have to decide right this minute. You want some time to think about it?" He had to give her at least that much of an out.

She squinted up at the sky, making Jesse wonder if she was consulting her grandmother or God or both. After a long minute, she held out her hand for the pen he was holding. "Nope. I don't need any more time. This is what I want. I want it to be perfect." She signed the proposal in a swirly, artistic hand.

This was going to be fun. In the end, they'd both end up with a showpiece—his to boast about to clients, hers to call home. Win-win, right? "Then the pursuit of perfect begins tomorrow afternoon."

Charlotte 1, Cottage 0.

Charlotte congratulated herself on the tiny victory her cup of tea represented.

A few days ago, the scorecard might have looked a lot more like Kitchen 1, Charlotte 0, but a visit from the electrician Jesse had recommended and two hours of vigilant scouring this morning had put the kitchen in working order. Stopping in at the local housewares store, Charlotte had purchased an electric kettle to hold her over until a wonderfully vintage-looking but thoroughly modern stove came in on special order. At another downtown boutique, she'd found a charming bistro table with two chairs. It felt so satisfying to buy things for the house, to launch the project that was coming to mean so much to her. It made her long-overdue Owner of Cottage tea on her back deck just about perfect. Add one of Mima's teacups and her favorite teapot, and life was wonderful.

See? I'm still here, she thought, smirking at the bright green leaves of the overhead tree. *I will not be beaten by this bump in the road.* "You know what Eleanor Roosevelt says," Charlotte addressed a gray squirrel that was perched on the deck railing with a quivering tail and greedy black eyes, peering at the bag of cookies she'd just opened. "Women are like tea bags—you never know how strong they are until you get them in hot water."

"Quoting first ladies to the wildlife, are we?" Jesse came around the corner of the house lugging a clanking canvas bag and an armful of cut lumber. "Look at you, having a proper tea on your back deck and all."

Charlotte laughed. "This is not a proper tea. It's barely even an improper tea."

Jesse settled his equipment on the bottom step, leaning against the railing to look up at her. "A Mulligan, then."

"A what?"

He grinned, looking so handsome that Charlotte was suddenly aware she was probably covered in kitchen grime. "You don't golf, do you?"

"Not even mini."

"A Mulligan is a do-over. The chance to retake a shot that went wrong."

Well, that certainly fit. "Yes, I suppose this is a Mulligan tea. I'd rather think of it as a victory lap. I'm declaring myself the winner in the epic battle of Charlotte versus the Filthy Kitchen." At least that was *one* thing she felt as though she'd won in this whole mess her life had become. "With a little backup from Mike the electrician, that is."

Jesse started rummaging through the canvas bag he had set down. "Mike made sure all your other appliances are going to work safely?"

"Everything's safe. He told me to tell you he's going to come back and do the upstairs bathroom wiring once you let him know the plaster is down."

Jesse's eyes lit up. "Demolition. My favorite part."

She cringed. "Somehow I'm not fond of the idea of you going at my bathroom with a sledgehammer." *My bathroom*. Funny how little things like that made her heart go *zing* today in a way that almost made up for her lack of incoming paychecks.

"Oh, I'm not going at it today." He held Charlotte's eyes for a dizzying moment. "You are."

Charlotte nearly toppled her teacup. "Me?"

"It's a thing of mine. First swing of demo always goes to the customer. If they're around, which you most definitely are."

"I'm sending a sledgehammer through my bathroom wall?" She'd seen such rituals on the home improvement networks, but she didn't think stuff like that actually took place on real jobs.

"Actually, it'll be more like a crowbar to the feet of your bathtub. Since you agreed to re-enamel it, I'm pulling it out today. Are you ready to start talking about color?"

Charlotte felt as if she'd been waiting a decade to pick the color of *something,* even though that was far from true. Colors—and how they went together—were a wondrous obsession for her, and part of the lure of the textile industry. Still, this choice felt new and exciting, in a way she couldn't quite define. She snatched the top issue from a pile of home decor magazines that were sitting next to the teapot. "I already have one picked out."

"Why am I not surprised?" Jesse walked up the last of the stairs. "Let's see."

She thumbed through the magazine to the dog-eared page, then held it up to Jesse to see. "That sink? The buttercream color with the brass fixtures? That's it, right there."

Jesse took the magazine. "Good choice. For a minute there I thought you were going to show me something purple or zebra striped. The guy who does the re-enameling work is good, but he's not a magician."

For a moment, Charlotte tried to imagine a zebra-striped claw-footed bathtub. Such a thing should never exist. "I have much better taste than animal prints for bathroom fixtures. He can do the sink to match, can't he?"

Jesse peered closer at the photograph. "It won't matter. You'll need a new sink no matter what—the newer fixtures won't fit on a sink like you've got. I'll bring you some catalogues with sinks that come in a color close to that tomorrow. When you pick the style and finish, Jack will make sure the bathtub matches perfectly." He looked up at her. "You're going to want one of those old-fashioned circle shower curtains, aren't you?"

"Absolutely. And in the brass finish. Not that cheap nickel finish."

"That brass finish is exactly that—not cheap. Are you sure?"

Parts of her were completely sure. Other parts—the edges of her chest that turned dark and trembling when she allowed herself to think of how her perfect life plan had been upended—balked at the extra price. Still, how many times in life did a girl get to pick out bathroom fixtures? Ones that would last for decades? A woman's bathroom was her sanctuary, her private escape from life's tensions. Hers *had* to be just right— especially when nothing else in life was. She nodded. Did he find that charming or annoying? His expression was unreadable, and she was growing a little nervous knot in her stomach. "I've even got the shower curtain and window treatment fabric picked out."

"You're going to be fun to work with, you know that?"

"I hope so." She really did. There was something so immensely satisfying about bringing the cottage back to life. As if the house had been waiting for her, holding its structural breath for her to come and pour her ideas inside. Charlotte had engineered some major achievements at Monarch, but those hadn't given her any security, had they? This cottage offered security, right down to the soul-nurturing buttercream color of her soon-to-be-reborn bathtub.

Jesse returned to his bag, making all kinds of rattling noises until he straightened back up with a crowbar, a pair of safety glasses and the daintiest pair of work gloves Charlotte had ever seen. Her astonishment must have shown all over her face, because Jesse waved the gloves and admitted, "These are from my mother. Don't ask."

She wanted to. The gloves were adorable, white canvas with a vintage-looking print of bright pink roses. They looked like garden gloves from a 1950s issue of *Better Homes and Gardens*. "I love them." Then, because she couldn't hold the curiosity in any longer, "Your mother sent these?"

He ran his hands down his face, but it didn't hide the flush she saw creep across his cheeks. "I said don't ask."

Charlotte pulled her knees up onto the chair and hugged them to her chest, utterly amused. "Do all your customers get adorable work gloves on their first day?" Jesse's mix of amusement and embarrassment was just too much fun to watch.

"Was there something about 'don't ask' that wasn't clear here? Or do you want me to take away your crowbar and just have at the bathtub on my own?"

"No!" she cried, leaping off her chair. The thought of starting, of finally getting this project underway, whizzed through her like electricity. She lunged for the gloves and the crowbar, but Jesse dodged her easily.

"Wait a minute, Ms. Taylor. If we're going to demo together, there are some rules. I can't have customers getting hurt on the job or letting their enthusiasm run away with their good sense."

Charlotte planted her hands on her hips and squared off against Jesse, even though he had a good six inches on her five-six frame. She raised her chin in defiance. "I never let my enthusiasm run away with my good sense."

The irony of that played out in Jesse's eyes the same moment her brain caught on to the idiocy of that statement made by an unemployed woman about to launch a major renovation project. He just raised one eyebrow, the corner of his mouth turning up in an unspoken, "Really?"

Charlotte used the distraction to pluck the crowbar from Jesse's hand. "Until now," she said, turning toward the door that led into what would be the dining room.

"Took the words right out of my mouth."

Chapter Five

Jesse watched Charlotte wiggle her fingers into the work gloves Mom had sent along. If they weren't so perfect for Charlotte, he'd have never agreed to something so unprofessional as a gift of fussy work gloves. Only these fit Charlotte's personality to a tee. Mom had won them in some social club raffle, and they were far too small for her arthritic hands, anyway. With a pang, Jesse wondered if Mom had been saving them for Randy's wife. Randy's ex-wife.

He'd wanted Constance and Randy to succeed, but even he could see she wasn't the sort of spouse who would continue to endure the kind of hours Randy kept. Jesse wanted his work to be a passion, surely, but not an obsession. That was part of why he loved the firehouse—it served as a constant reminder that there was more to life than a paycheck. There was a certain poetic justice in spending his work hours constructing when so much of the firefighting battled destruction.

Charlotte's wide-spread and wiggling floral fingers pulled his thoughts back to the present. He should have remembered pulling the bathtub would be a tight squeeze in this narrow bathroom—he was so close to her he could smell the flowers in whatever lotion she wore. Something sweet but with just a bit of zing, like her personality. Jesse held out the clunky safety glasses. "Time to accessorize."

He hadn't counted on her looking so adorable, standing there like an enthusiastic fish with those big brown eyes filling the gogglelike lenses. Her smile was beyond distracting, and she looked so utterly happy. He'd been grumpy for days after he "lost" the cottage—for that matter he got grumpy when he lost a basketball game at the firehouse—but she managed to keep her bounce even when losing her job, not to mention her beloved grandmother. What about her made that kind of resilience possible?

He straddled the antiquated pipes that ran up one side of the bathtub, pulling a wrench from his tool belt to detach them from the floor. Best to get to work right away before the urge to stare at her made him do something stupid. Well, stupider than presenting her with fussy gloves and a baby crowbar. "Pry up that flange while I pull from here."

"Flange?"

Yep, stupider. More every minute. "The circle thing around the bottom of the pipe. Wedge the crowbar into the waxy stuff holding it to the tile and yank it free."

She was a parade of different emotions as she got down on her knees and thrust the crowbar under the seal. Anxiety, determination, excitement, worry—they seemed to flash across her face in split-second succession. He liked that she was so emotionally invested in the place, but it bugged him how transparent her feelings seemed to him. "Go on," he encouraged, charmed by the way she bit her lip and the "ready or not" look in her wide eyes. "You can do this."

Charlotte gave the fixtures a determined glare, then got down on her knees and thrust the crowbar under the seal. The yelp of victory she gave when the suction gave way and the ring sprang up off the tile to clatter against the pipe was—and he was going to have to find a way to stop using this word—adorable. She brandished the crowbar as she sat back on her haunches and watched him go through the process of unhooking the bathtub from its plumbing. He could have done this alone more quickly—maybe even more easily—but this was too much fun. Getting this porcelain behemoth down the stairs to his truck would be the exact opposite of fun, but he'd called in a few guys from the firehouse to help with that, even though they wouldn't add to the scenery the way Charlotte's grin currently did.

She ran a hand along the lip of the deep tub. "Mima would have loved this tub. You were smart to talk me into saving it."

The expensive Jacuzzi model she'd had her eye on seemed like a ridiculous indulgence he would have talked anyone out of buying. Especially when this one could be so easily repaired. "Tell me about her." The question seemed to jump from his mouth, surprising her as much as it did him.

Her eyes lit up with affection. "Mima? She was 'a piece of work,' Grandpa always used to say. Her real name was Naomi Charlotte Dunning, but when I was little I couldn't quite say Naomi, so I just said 'Mi' at first. Then it became 'Mima' and that stuck. I'm named after her. She was a great woman. Grandpa had Alzheimer's like Melba's dad, and Mima was a hero in how she took care of him. When he died, I know she grieved and was scared to go on without him, but she found her courage. So much so that she decided to scatter some of his ashes all over the world. And I mean all over the world. She'd been on almost every continent, and left a little bit of Grandpa everywhere she went." She shrugged. "It's hopelessly romantic, isn't it?"

"I guess." He was pretty sure his parents had already purchased grave plots at the local cemetery and probably had a file somewhere with precise instructions as to what was going to go on their markers. Dad was a firm believer in advance planning, which was why he was so quick to categorize Jesse's career as "unfocused."

Charlotte sighed. "I want to be just like that when I'm her age. I'd want to be just like that now, if I could."

Jesse couldn't think of a single family member— not even Mom—he would praise like that. Family just didn't spur that kind of adoration in his world. "Did you spend a lot of time with her?"

"Tons. She took me on a few of her earlier, smaller trips. Now I get...well—" she swallowed hard "—I *used* to get postcards from her adventures."

He hardly even needed to ask. "And you kept them, didn't you?"

"I'm going to buy beautiful silver frames for all of them and fill the dining room wall."

She had plans—ambitious plans—for every room in the house. Jesse knew a thing or two about dreaming up plans. It made him wonder where he'd be right now if he had half the determination Charlotte had to put hers in play the way she did. "That will be nice."

Charlotte leaned in, pushing the safety goggles up on top of her head. "I loved her travels, but even when Mima wasn't going anywhere, she was great. You know those teenage years, when you think your parents are the world's worst? I would hang out at Mima's house and declare my life a disaster, and she would just sit there in her rocking chair with her knitting and let me rant. That's where I learned to knit—from Mima. She'd take me to the yarn store and buy me whatever I wanted—even crazy colors or wild novelty yarns— and then we'd go home and make something amazing with it together."

Jesse yanked the first of the two water pipes free and started on the second. "My grandmother taught me her beef stew recipe, but it wasn't quite the warm, fuzzy experience you described."

She cocked her head, sending the glasses askew so that she had to catch them with her hand. "What do you mean?"

"It was less of an 'I'm passing down the family recipe' thing and more of a 'Don't you mess this up and besmirch the Sykes family name' thing. She had no granddaughters, so I think I was just a stand-in. My brother's marriage didn't last long enough to permit any recipe sharing with his wife, anyway." He pointed to the claw foot of the tub nearest his foot. "Ready to pry that up?"

"I won't break it, will I?"

"This is a two-hundred-pound hunk of coated metal. I doubt you could even chip it."

"But it's cracked already." She really had become attached to the thing. It was a bathroom fixture, for crying out loud, not a family heirloom.

"You'll be fine." Because she looked so worried he added, "Just go slow and stop when I tell you."

That foot and the next came free easily, and Jesse was able to angle the tub out of the alcove where it sat and pry up the last two feet with no trouble at all. Once he'd turned the tub away from the wall, the offending crack could be seen. Charlotte ran her finger down the rusted crack, giving a little groan as if she was dressing a wound. "This can be fixed, can't it?"

Jesse made the mistake of hunching down beside her on the narrow floor. It put them too close. "I'm almost positive. The rust isn't that bad and my guy is an artist."

She ran her hands along the top again. "You know, now I'm glad we're saving her. It'd be a shame to ditch such a beautiful old thing just for a few hotshot Jacuzzi jets, don't you think?"

He shot her a look. "You realize you're talking about a bathtub, right? You're not gonna give it a name or anything. Are you?" Boats, pets and people got names—not bathtubs—but the way Charlotte was looking, he couldn't be sure.

The corner of her mouth turned up. "I'm not the crazy lady who names her plants and has a dozen cats. Not yet, at least. I do plan to own a cat in the near future, though, so you never know."

Jesse chose not to hide his grimace. "A cat?" Maybe he could talk her into holding off until the renovation was complete. Surely he could scour the internet for home construction cat dangers and tell a few horror stories to warn her off.

Charlotte sat back against the wall and crossed her arms over her chest. "Well, if I didn't already guess you to be a dog person, I now have conclusive proof."

"I always heard cats and yarn were a bad combination." He began dismantling the hot and cold faucets from the end of the tub. "You know, jigsaw puzzle photos of kittens tangled up in yarn balls and all."

"I'll take my chances. I'm too enamored of my shoe collection to risk the damage a puppy could do." As if it had suddenly occurred to her, she asked, "How on earth are you going to get this thing down the stairs?"

Jesse checked his watch. "A few of the guys from the firehouse will be here in twenty minutes. I should have all these fixtures removed in ten minutes, and then we can start on the sink. That we can just whack apart with a sledgehammer."

Her eyes popped. "You're not really—"

"No." She really was too much fun to mess with. "Unless you want to?"

It was the most amusing thing to watch. She was frightened of taking a hammer to her bathroom walls, but there was this corner of her eyes that lit up with the idea. The way that woman could run away with his practicality was going to be very dangerous, indeed. *Keep your distance, Sykes—the last thing you need to do is mess this up.*

"And then he took the sink out onto the driveway. I took that great big hammer, hoisted it over my head and split that sink into two pieces right there." Charlotte felt the ear-to-ear grin return, just as it had every time she remembered the sensation of cracking that sink right down the middle. "I didn't know I had it in me."

"I didn't know you had it in you, either." Melba laughed. "Honestly, I can't picture it. Sounds rather unsafe."

"No, Jesse brought me safety glasses and gloves and everything." She leaned closer to the circle of wide-eyed women at the Gordon Falls Community Church knitting group. "But I think even he was a little shocked that I broke it in half on my first try. The firehouse guys, when they came to help drag the tub down the stairs and into Jesse's truck? They were impressed. Guess all that upper-body work at the gym paid off. I'm telling you, it's satisfying. Demolition therapy is seriously underutilized."

The women all looked shocked—all except for Violet Sharpton, an elderly woman with a sweet expression and a quirky personality. She looked almost envious. "What fun!"

"It made me feel a little bit powerful." In fact, it had made her feel like a momentary superhero, a great memory to pull out when the surges of panic came. "For a woman in a job search, a little confidence boost goes a long way."

"Speaking of a confidence boost," said Melba, "show them your shawl, Charlotte. I want the ladies to see how really talented you are."

Charlotte reached into her knitting bag and produced a sky-blue shawl of mohair-silk lace. Stitched from a knitting pattern and yarn Mima had brought back from Ireland, Charlotte considered this shawl a personal masterpiece.

"Wow. You weren't kidding, Melba. That's beautiful!" Tina, one of the older ladies of the group, ran her fingers across the intricate stitch work.

"I told you, she's talented," Melba boasted. "Look at that lace work."

Charlotte held up the shawl. "It looks hard, but it's really not that complicated."

Violet somehow managed a friendly frown. "Didn't your mother ever teach you to hush up and accept a compliment? It may be easy for you, but some of us would never make it through the first inch." The older woman looked around the room to her fellow knitters. "Can you imagine how blessed someone's going to be when they get even a basic shawl knit with that kind of talent?" The purpose of the group was to make prayer shawls, hand-knitted wraps that were prayed over and given to people in need of healing or comfort. Charlotte had sent supplies from Monarch when Melba first started the group. "Thanks to Charlotte," Violet continued, "I think we've just taken things up a notch around here."

Melba looked pleased the group had taken so quickly to Charlotte. "You all remember it was Charlotte who set us up when I began to teach you all how to knit." Charlotte was pleased, too, feeling right at home in a matter of minutes. She'd always been that way with knitters—she could walk into a yarn shop anywhere in the world and feel as though she was among friends.

Her new friends all narrowed their eyes, evidently feeling the injustice of Charlotte's job loss as much as she did. "They shouldn't have let you go," Violet said. "It's a crying shame, that's what I say, even if Chicago's loss is our gain. Still, you seem a smart cookie to me. You'll land on your feet in no time."

Charlotte wondered whether she ought to admit she said something similar to herself in the bathroom mirror every morning, pep-talking herself into facing another day of unanswered queries and diminishing funds. Instead, she just quoted something Mima always said, "From your mouth to God's ears."

"That's right," another woman, Abby Reed, chimed in. "You've got yourself one powerful posse of prayer warriors on your side now. These ladies know how to storm the gates of heaven, I tell you."

"Good thing," Charlotte admitted as she began stitching. *Stitch,* she told herself. *Don't complain or whine, just stitch. Look confident and you'll be confident.*

"I admire you." Tina turned her knitting to start a new row. "Not too many folks your age would see the value in buying a home and setting down roots while you're still single. Shows confidence, independence, common sense—all those good 'ence' words."

"You should talk to my Ben." Abby groaned. "Since he graduated he hasn't shown any of those words except *nonsense.* You'd think a job was going to land gift-wrapped in his lap the way he lollygags around the house. Frank has threatened to force him onto the fire department in another two weeks if the boy doesn't step things up."

Violet held up the navy blue shawl she was working on, a textured piece with white stripes down the side. Melba had told her Violet was one of the newer knitters, but Charlotte would have never known it by the woman's work—she was a natural. "Think we could pray some sense into this and give it to him?"

Abby laughed. "You'd be better off praying some patience into one and wrapping it over my mouth. We keep fighting over this. I was so excited to have him back home from college, but I'll tell you the novelty has worn off."

"You were saying you needed more staff at the shop," Marge Bowers suggested. "Can't he work there?" Abby ran the town gift shop, which also stocked a small selection of locally produced yarn. Charlotte had been in there numerous times—she wasn't a parent, but it didn't take a genius to know it wasn't a place most young men would ever want to work.

Jeannie Owens balked. "Can you see Ben making sales in Abby's shop? The only thing worse would be having him selling my candy—he'd eat all my profits."

"I thought about sending him over to bag at Halverson's Grocery just to get the employee discount—that boy eats enough for five people!"

Violet pointed her free needle at Abby. "You should do that. The bag boys at Halverson's don't show a lick of sense these days. Might do them good to have a college graduate in their midst."

"I just hope they motivate Ben to find a job that actually uses that expensive accounting degree." Abby looked up from her knitting. "Hey, this is sounding like a better idea every minute."

Charlotte let her gaze wander from face to friendly face. How often had she told Melba that this was what she loved about Gordon Falls? The people shared things, getting through life side by side, warts and all. These were the women who had held Melba up during the long, painful decline of her father's Alzheimer's. They'd held her friend close when he'd finally passed away, so much so that Charlotte never worried for Melba's support when she couldn't make it out to Gordon Falls. Why, then, did she resist telling them—and Melba— how frightening being jobless was to her? *End this wait, Lord,* Charlotte finished her row of stitching as she sent a silent prayer for God's favor over the dozen electronic résumés she'd sent out earlier this morning. *Send me a job.*

"Charlotte, if you could have any job in the world, what would it be?" Jeannie, who filled a room with sunny-eyed optimism wherever she went despite a host of personal challenges, posed the question as she poured herself a second cup of coffee.

"Oh, naturally, I've always thought about opening a yarn shop. I might do it someday, but I know enough to realize how much work it is."

Jeannie and Abby, both small business owners, nodded in agreement.

"I'm still looking to work for someone, to let all the

managerial headaches be on someone else's plate for a while longer," Charlotte added.

She thought about Jesse. After they wrestled the bathtub free, she'd managed to get him to open up about his plans to launch his own business. He seemed pretty autonomous as it was, despite working for Mondale Construction, but was bursting with the urge to work for himself and call his own shots. She admired his ambition, but she could also see the dark edge of it. Jesse wanted success to show the world that he could do it, to prove himself worthy. From a few side comments he'd made, she suspected his father had a lot to do with that drive—and not in a good way. She was so fortunate to have Mom and Dad, who believed in her no matter what she did. When she owned her own business, it would be for all the right reasons. For now, it was enough that she owned her own cottage.

Chapter Six

"You've made quite an impression," Charlotte's cousin JJ announced when they ran into each other a few days later at Halverson's Grocery. This was another small-town phenomenon that still startled Charlotte—a trip to the grocery store turned into a social event every time. She'd yet to fill her basket without running into six or seven people she knew—not to mention being introduced to half a dozen new "neighbors." That certainly never happened at the city convenience mart.

"Jesse's account of your powerhouse sink demolition was the talk of the firehouse," JJ went on, as the two of them wandered down the frozen-food aisle. "As if your first-day kitchen fire hadn't endeared you to the guys already."

"I think I was hoping for less fanfare tied to my entrance into Gordon Falls," Charlotte admitted. "The past few months have been a bit more dramatic than I'd like."

"Well, if you're not into drama, you've hired the wrong guy. Jesse Sykes is as Hollywood as they come. You remember him singing at our wedding, don't you?"

Just the other afternoon she was upstairs measuring windows when Jesse either forgot she was home or didn't care that she heard him. His voice echoed stunningly throughout the empty house, and she'd stopped to lean against the wall and just listen. Smooth as silk and soulful to boot. Mima would have declared Jesse to have "a set of pipes" and Charlotte had to agree. "He's amusing, and he's got a great voice, that's for sure."

JJ's voice softened. "He's a great guy. A bit of a loose cannon sometimes, but a heart of gold." She grinned. "Mostly." When Charlotte narrowed one eye at her she added, "You could do worse."

She really didn't want to get into this with JJ again. Her cousin knew her concerns about getting involved with a first responder without them arguing it out for the umpteenth time. Anyway, it felt wrong to tell one firefighter that you didn't think you could do life alongside another firefighter. "Sure, he's got personality. He's not for me, though."

Was there anyone out there for her? She liked to think so, though she was getting frustrated waiting for him to show up. In any case, now wasn't the time for a new relationship. Now should be about being her own person, stepping confidently—if not smoothly—into the future God had for her. Dating would just muck up her thinking and add to her anxiety. And really, the last thing she needed right now was the prospect of any more rejection.

"I thought you just said he was amusing." JJ selected a bag of frozen peas and placed them in her cart.

"Amusement is not the same thing as attraction." That felt dishonest, because she did feel an attraction to Jesse. She just knew better than to act on it. "I'll admit, we're having a bit of fun with this renovation project, and I could sure use a bit of fun right now, but that's all. Besides, from the little I heard, he's got all kinds of family baggage and I don't need anyone like that."

"Who's got family baggage?" Melba and Maria came up the aisle, waving hello. *Here we go again, a party in the frozen-food aisle.* It had its fun side, but Charlotte fretted her days of throwing on sweats and a baseball hat to duck into the grocery store were over.

"Sykes," JJ replied.

Melba sighed. "Everyone's got family baggage of some kind."

"Maybe, but your family baggage is adorable." JJ wiggled one of Maria's irresistible tiny pink toes, making the baby girl giggle.

"What would Mima have thought of Jesse?" JJ asked, surrendering the toe as, with the astounding flexibility of babies, Maria pulled it up to stuff it in her mouth. All three women laughed. Even though JJ and Max were Charlotte's cousins on her father's side, Mima left a big enough impression that both sides of Charlotte's relatives knew and loved the woman. Max and JJ had come to Mima's funeral, and not just because they wanted to support Charlotte and her parents.

Mima's opinion of Jesse—or what it would have been—was an interesting point to consider. Charlotte had to think for a moment, biding her time as she filled her own handbasket with a box of frozen breakfast sandwiches. "Hard to say. She'd like his sense of humor, but I doubt she'd have found him artistic enough."

"Your grandmother always was a pushover for the poetic types, judging from the way your grandfather won her over," Melba offered, gently removing the toe from Maria's drool-soaked mouth. "It's got to be too early for teething, doesn't it?"

JJ and Charlotte shrugged. Charlotte noticed a new weariness in Melba's voice and eyes.

"I still think you should publish all those love letters as a book," Melba went on. "Your grandfather was a heart slayer on the page in his day." The new mother sighed. "Nobody does that sort of romantic stuff anymore."

Charlotte leaned over and tickled Maria. "Is my darling goddaughter cutting into Mommy's love life?"

Melba's sigh turned into a yawn. "Right behind the firehouse. Between Clark's days and Maria's nights, I'm stretched to the limit. This parenting stuff is hard."

"The chief has been wound pretty tight these days, too," JJ added.

Charlotte eyed her friend. "When's the last time you and Clark had an evening to yourselves?"

Melba's only response was a sad smile. "It's worth it."

JJ put a hand on Melba's sagging shoulder. "You two deserve to be off duty. No offense, but you look exhausted. And honestly I could use a less grumpy boss."

"That's it, I'm babysitting." Charlotte pulled out her smartphone to check her calendar. There was nothing like helping others to get her mind off her own problems. And she adored Maria. *This should be a fun task.* "When is the next night Clark has free?"

Melba rolled her eyes. "Who knows?"

"Clark does," said JJ. "Text him right now and ask him."

"Right now?" Melba seemed more interested in the choice of green beans, and that was bad news in the romance department.

Charlotte shut the freezer cabinet door in front of

Melba's face. "This instant. You're outnumbered three to one."

"Three?"

"Maria agrees with me."

Two minutes and a package of ground turkey later, Melba peered at her phone and declared, "Thursday night."

"Mission accomplished. Okay, ladies, I have to get going." JJ's face took on a glow. "Alex is heading out of town again, and I promised him one home-cooked meal before he gets on another plane."

Melba gazed after the lovestruck firefighter and then pushed out a breath as she deposited a box of biscuit mix into her cart. "I'm pretty sure Clark and I looked that smitten once."

"Exactly my point," Charlotte replied. "I'm baby-sitting next Thursday night so you and Chief Bradens can have some time to rekindle your flame."

"I'm likely to fall asleep at the restaurant table," Melba admitted. "I can't remember the last time I sat down for a whole meal. They don't call 5:00 p.m. 'the fussing hour' for nothing. By the time Clark pulls in the driveway I'm ready to take a hot bath and tell the world good-night. At least until Maria wakes up again."

The strain in her friend's eyes tugged at Charlotte's heart. Melba had been through so much since moving to Gordon Falls—the long, hard struggle to care for her father, his eventual death—she'd thanked God for sending Clark to Melba a million times over the past year. And now baby Maria added more joy to their lives, but they were both clearly tired. While Melba never complained, Charlotte knew being married to the fire chief wasn't the easiest job in the world. Dad had been only a police captain, and it had taken a lot out of Mom. She touched Melba's elbow. "You need this. Let me do this for you. It's one night. Even if Maria screams the entire time, I can handle it."

Jesse set down the nozzles he was cleaning a few days later and stared at Chief Bradens. "Really?"

Chief nodded. "With your background, you never thought about taking the inspector's training?"

"Well, no." Fire inspectors were career guys. The Gordon Falls department had only two paid employees, Chief Bradens himself and the fire inspector, Chad Owens. While some volunteer guys looked to shift to a paid professional post, Jesse never counted himself among them. As his father never missed a chance to point out, this job asked enough of him on a volunteer basis. He wasn't eager to expand that. "Chad's not retiring or anything, is he?"

"Not that he's told me. It's just that I see the potential in you."

"I don't know. Sounds like a whole lot of paper pushing to me." Chad spent more time at a desk than on a truck, and Jesse knew enough of the Gordon Falls building codes to know they could tax a guy's patience. "I'm allergic to administrative tasks."

The chief leaned up against the truck that sat parked behind where Jesse was working. "I thought you wanted to own your own business someday."

"I do."

"You'll have to get over your allergic reaction to paperwork."

Jesse gave a grunt. "Mondale doesn't do paperwork."

"That's because his wife does his billing and filing. You planning to marry into an administrative family anytime soon?"

Jesse tried to scowl, but his brain went straight to Charlotte's thick, color-coded files of renovation ideas. "No."

Too late. Chief Bradens leaned in. "And what was that?"

"What was what?"

"That look."

"What look?" Jesse turned his attention to the box of nozzles, only to have the chief kick them out from under his grasp.

"Melba tells me you've been spending a lot of time at Charlotte Taylor's cottage."

Jesse knew the connection between Charlotte and the Bradens was going to tangle him up soon, but he hadn't counted on it wrapping around him quite this fast. "It's a big job. I'm glad for the work."

"Melba thinks you might be glad for the client."

How was he supposed to answer that? "She's nice."

Clark leaned down to meet Jesse's eyes. "She is. Charlotte is a great person. She's Melba's best friend and they've been through a lot together. She's Maria's godmother."

"I know she's a friend of yours. I've been trying to do right by her because of it. I told you that."

"And I appreciate it. I do. I just want to be sure you know to tread carefully here."

Jesse raised himself up from the box. "Meaning?"

"Meaning I'd want the department's most confirmed bachelor not to stomp on the heart of my wife's best friend. She's in a vulnerable spot, and subtlety isn't your strong suit."

Jesse chose his words carefully. "Is that a command to steer clear, Chief?" While Clark Bradens was a caring leader and Jesse considered him something of a mentor, he usually kept a clean line between personal and firehouse business.

Bradens's expression softened. "I can't tell you how to spend your personal time. But I know you and I know Charlotte. I'm asking you, as a friend and as chief, to be careful. Charlotte doesn't do halfway or casual—and I've never known you to do anything but. If you choose to go after her, I'd want to know you really mean it."

"Hey, no worries there. I'm not going after her." She did intrigue him, but there were lots of reasons to leave that alone for now. Like Chief said, he needed to keep his relationships halfway and casual right now. Charlotte was a client. She was a bit too artsy for his taste. And then there was the subject of Sunday mornings. "I don't think I spend enough time in church to be her type anyhow."

The chief's expression made Jesse regret his choice of reply. "You can change that if you want. The congregation talent show is soon, and we're still looking for an emcee."

That made Jesse laugh. "Me? Master of ceremonies at the GFCC talent night? Don't you think that's a bit ridiculous?"

"Have you ever seen our talent show?" Bradens smirked. "Ridiculous is nearly a requirement. It's the talent that seems to be optional."

"Why don't *you* do it?"

"I'll have to if I don't find someone else. This year providing the emcee is the firehouse's contribution. We could really use someone who has some actual theatrical tendencies."

Sure, he was a born show-off, but Jesse still shook his head. "I think I'll pass."

"Will you at least think about it? That, and the inspector's training?"

Some days Bradens just didn't know the meaning of the word *no*. "Yeah, fine, I'll give it some thought. I doubt I'll change my mind, though, so keep looking for someone else."

"You're my first choice. On both fronts. Just know that, okay?"

Both of those fronts, but not first choice for Charlotte, huh? That stung just a little, but suited him fine, anyway. "Sure, okay."

Chapter Seven

Charlotte was regretting her final "I can handle it" words to Melba. It was eight-thirty, and Maria hadn't stopped crying since Melba went out the door at six. Charlotte had fed her, changed her, rocked her and done just about every other baby-soothing thing she could think of, but still Maria wailed.

"All right, Maria, it's a nice night, so you and I are going to go for a walk. Any more of your cries bouncing off the walls in this house and I'm going to go a little bonkers. If the river doesn't soothe you, nothing will."

Charlotte found the stroller (complete with an adorable hand-knit baby blanket) on the back porch, penned a quick note and stuck it to the fridge—all one-handed because the red-faced Maria occupied the other arm—and headed out into the warm June night.

Gordon Falls was at its best on summer evenings. The town spread itself out along the Gordon River, filling the hillsides with quaint homes and dotting the town's main thoroughfare of Tyler Street with a collection of charming shops and restaurants. It was a picture-postcard small town. Charlotte had joked about the overwhelming quaintness of the place on her first visit, but she'd come to really love the community. It was as far away from the hustle and concrete of Chicago as she could get, and she could always feel her stress peeling off her soul as her car pulled through the big green floodgates that stood at the edge of Tyler Street. Even Maria simmered down to a steady whimper punctuated by a few bursts of crying.

Charlotte headed toward Tyler Street and the far end of Riverwalk, sure to be filled with people enjoying the evening but far enough from the restaurant where Clark and Melba were dining so that she wouldn't risk running into them. She already had a host of memories connected to places in town: the housewares store where she'd purchased the new kettle. The hardware store where she'd gotten her first spare set of keys made. The grocery store where she seemed to meet everyone she knew on every visit. The boutique that was sure to be her favorite place for clothes—once she spent time and energy on clothes instead of curtains. Abby Reed's craft and gift store, which held just enough yarn to make Charlotte feel as though she hadn't abandoned all artistic civilization. She hadn't been back to her Chicago apartment in almost three weeks, and she hadn't even missed it. That place was boxy, ordinary and noisy. The cottage was on its way to becoming quiet, filled with charm and a thing of beauty to help the rest of life's stress disappear.

What are You up to, Lord? Why am I so drawn to this place? Charlotte wondered to God as she pushed a fussing Maria through the town. *I've never felt a place could make me so happy before this. It's always been people that made me happy. Only now I've lost my colleagues and Mima. The things here—the things in my house, even—are what make me happiest now. Is that wrong? Or just different?* Charlotte looked down at Maria's frustrated mad-at-the-world pout and thought, *Kiddo, I know how you feel.*

Her Tyler Street journeys led her down by the firehouse and Karl's Koffee. It wouldn't hurt to meet a friendlier face than Maria's frustrated red cheeks and tiny balled fists.

Maria's wailing ensured that most people heard her coming before they saw her. Two grandmother-types outside of Karl's had offered some tactics, but neither of them had worked, and Charlotte admitted to growing a little anxious that maybe her goddaughter was suffering from something more than simple fussiness. It wasn't much of a surprise that Maria's cries caught the ears of the firefighters on duty as Charlotte walked by.

"Hey, is that the Charlotte?" A stocky man from the firehouse called as he rose from his lawn chair on the driveway.

Charlotte stopped, startled that he'd called her by name. "Um, hi."

A younger fireman—in actual red suspenders, Charlotte noted with amusement—came out from behind one of the bright red trucks that stood ready in their enormous garage spaces. "Yorky, you gotta stop calling Chief Bradens's kid 'the chieflette.'" He wiped his hands on a towel that he subsequently stuffed into a back pocket. "Chieflette's not a name. It's not even a real word. It's just weird."

He hadn't been saying "Charlotte"—he'd been saying "chieflette." Charlotte felt a twinge of satisfaction that the baby's firehouse nickname sounded so close to her own. After a second she remembered Yorky from her ill-fated first day as cottage owner.

He was currently balking at the younger guy. "Everybody in here has a nickname, why not the baby?" His eyes popped in recognition. "Hey, you're the cottage lady."

"I am." She held out her hand. "Charlotte. And I think 'chieflette' is kind of cute. It's certainly original." Which kindled a fierce curiosity as to what name Jesse had been given. Smiling at Yorky, she made a mental note to discover a sneaky way to find out. Maria gave a wail of disapproval as if to counteract her godmother's endorsement.

"She's certainly cranky." Yorky peered into the stroller. "Gas?"

Charlotte sighed and picked Maria up out of the stroller to settle her against her shoulder. "I've burped her. Twice. Some lady even tried some special colic hold outside of Karl's, but nothing seems to help."

"Is she running a fever?" The younger man went to reach for Maria's head, but Yorky swatted his hand away.

"Wash your hands before you touch a baby, son—everybody knows that." When the man pulled the towel back out from his pocket, Yorky frowned. "And no, that's not enough." For a big, burly guy, Yorky was evidently a softie for babies. "Shame JJ's not on tonight—women always have a knack for that stuff."

If women always have a knack for this, why am I pushing a screaming baby down Tyler Street? Charlotte thought, suddenly fighting a wave of insecurity. She tried to give an educated touch to Maria's forehead. "No fever that I can tell."

"Go see if Pipes is still here," Yorky said to his companion, cocking his head back toward the firehouse kitchen window.

"He left an hour ago. Him and Wally are grilling out down by the river with some of the probies."

Pipes? Probies? Some days firemen seemed to speak a different language. "Is Pipes a parent?"

That brought a guffaw from Yorky. "Jesse? Now wouldn't that be a hoot. Nah, Jesse's just got silver pipes. The guy sings to kids when they're scared from the fires. Honestly, it'd be hard to keep him around if he weren't so good at it."

So Jesse's nickname was "Pipes." The singing she'd heard echoing through her house certainly validated the name. Jesse's silky voice struck her as a Frank Sinatra–Harry Connick Jr.–Michael Bublé sort of croon, but with a decidedly soulful edge. Based on the wails she'd been enduring for the past pair of hours, getting Jesse to sing Maria to sleep seemed like the best idea in the world. "I'll go find him, if you don't mind. Where on the riverwalk is he?"

"Just south of the footbridge. Go a block farther than Karl's Koffee and you should be able to smell the meat burning."

Maria gave a yowl as if she was working up to another good fit again, spurring Charlotte to settle the fussy baby back into the stroller and turn them both toward the river. She'd pledged to herself to do anything necessary to present Melba and Clark with a happy baby when they got home from dinner—those two deserved some peace and quiet. They deserved to not feel one pang of guilt for taking an evening to themselves. "Thanks, I'm sure I'll find him."

"He'll probably hear you coming," Yorky offered with an understanding smile. "But I can page him if you like."

"No, I think we can make it to the footbridge in one

piece. Thanks, Yorky." She took an immediate liking to the stocky, middle-aged firefighter. He was a big bear of a man with a heart of butter—who wouldn't like a man with that smile? "And extra thanks—you know—for playing hero the other day at my cottage."

"Nothin' doing, Charlotte. That's why we're here. You just take care of the little chieflette there and we'll call it even."

Charlotte started walking toward the river. "Chieflette, huh? You could do worse, Maria. You've got two dozen uncles looking out after you, little lady. That's good, because with those red curls and that smile—the one you haven't shown me in hours, I might add—you're gonna need 'em."

"Aw," Wally groaned as he bit into his hamburger. "Aw, Sykes, this is carnivore perfection." He wiped a smear of Sykes's Special Sauce from his chin, a look of gastronomic pleasure on his face. "What's in here?"

Jesse smiled as he passed off a burger to another firefighter in training, or "probie," as they were known around the firehouse. "Wouldn't you like to know."

To be known for an awesome burger was a small satisfaction, but Jesse liked the appreciation. The firehouse boasted only three decent cooks, so meals were a gamble most nights. If they ever went to a professional model where the firefighters lived on-site in regular shifts, it'd become a serious issue. As it was with rotating shifts of volunteers on call, meals were more of a perk than a requirement. Jesse liked to make sure he was around on Thursday nights when the butcher always sent over burgers. It was a crime to see good meat destroyed by bad cooks.

A sharp cry caught his ear as he slid his spatula

under the final burger and handed it off to another grateful probie. There was a baby nearby, and an unhappy one at that.

Jesse put the cover back on the grill and wiped the spatula clean on a towel. He dipped a finger in the plastic bowl of Sykes's Special Sauce, licking a tangy taste before snapping the lid into place. Man, that stuff was delicious. Maybe someday he'd consider bottling it and selling it wholesale to bars and burger joints. His thoughts were interrupted as the high-pitched wail grew louder, and he turned to see the source of the drama.

It was Charlotte Taylor. Chief Bradens had mentioned she was babysitting his daughter tonight. The strained look on Charlotte's face told him it wasn't going well.

He left the bowl on the table and walked toward the noisy pair. "Somebody having a rough night?"

"She's been like this for almost two hours. I've tried everything I know and a few things complete strangers have suggested." Charlotte pushed her hair back from her face in exasperation. "In another hour I'll be ready to cry myself."

Jesse reached back to the table to pull an antiseptic wipe from a container and used it to clean the last of barbecue and Sykes's Sauce off his hands. "I'll bet."

"Smells great." Charlotte nodded toward the grill with a weak attempt at a smile. Poor thing, she really did look at the end of her rope.

"Just gave out the last one, sorry."

"No, I've eaten. I just didn't realize your skill set included cooking."

"Oh, it sure does," one young man said with a mouth full of burger. "Sure does."

"It's nice to have an appreciative audience," Jesse

admitted, peering into the stroller to see a puffy red face surrounded by a halo of Bradens-red curls. "Seems Chieflette's got a temper to match her locks."

Charlotte laughed. "I heard Yorky call her that." She gave Jesse a slightly panicked look. "I also heard they don't call you Pipes for nothing and that you're great at calming down kids. Care to work some of that vocal medicine on Little Miss Fussbudget here?" She looked just short of desperate.

It was the chief's baby. It was Charlotte asking. What kind of fool would say no? "No guarantees, but I'll do my best." A surprising knot settled in Jesse's stomach. Normally he was never given to nerves—especially about singing—but for some reason the stakes felt higher at the moment. Distracting five-year-olds at the preschool fire drill was one thing. Soothing a fussy baby in front of a pack of probies and Charlotte Taylor? Well, that was quite another. "Okay," he said, infusing his voice with confidence he didn't fully feel, "hand Little Miss Crankypants over and let's see if we can calm her down."

At first, Maria didn't care at all to be handed over to a strange set of arms. As he settled her against his shoulder, she wailed, and out of the corner of his eye Jesse saw Charlotte wringing her hands. Starting down in as low a register as he could manage, Jesse launched into a slow, soft version of Ben E. King's "Stand by Me." He remembered reading somewhere that the rumble of a deep voice in a chest was soothing to babies. When that didn't have much of an effect, he modulated up a key and began to sway around the grass with her, holding her tight and patting her back the way he'd seen his grandmother do. Halfway into the second chorus, Maria gave a little hiccup and softened her wails.

A natural tenor, Jesse was more comfortable in

higher keys, and the tiny bit of progress he'd made bolstered his confidence. He was "Pipes," and while he mostly used his voice for laughs, he also knew this was his gift, the particular talent he brought to firefighting. He could serenade somebody calm in the back of an ambulance, as they made their way down the ladder or as they waited for their loved ones to emerge from a smoking building. And, okay, he was a bit of a born show-off. Showing off for a good cause like helping Charlotte help Chief Bradens? Well, that ought to be a cakewalk. When Maria calmed further, Jesse took it up another key and began dancing with Maria. He caught Charlotte's eye, winked and spun Maria in a tiny turn that actually produced a sigh from the baby.

"Will you look at that?" one of the probies said with astonished eyes. "It's like he's the baby whisperer or something."

By the third chorus, Jesse had produced an actual laugh from Maria. Well, at least it sounded like a laugh. He ignored the growing wet spot on his shoulder, focusing instead on the steady small breaths coming under his hand on Maria's back. By the end of the second song, Maria was out cold, Charlotte was astonished and Jesse felt downright victorious. He'd sung victims to calm—or something at least close to reasonable—before, but he'd never actually sung a baby to sleep. There was a startling satisfaction in the accomplishment, which fueled a warm glow under his ribs. Very, very carefully, he lowered a contented Maria back into the stroller and then looked up to catch Charlotte's wide smile.

"Better keep walking so she stays asleep," one of the probies said behind him.

Jesse turned, head cocked in annoyance. "If you

know so much about babies, Carson, why wait until now to speak up?"

"Hey," Carson replied, "I'm the oldest of eight. But no way was I going to step in and miss a chance to see the Great Sykes at work. Just keep walking for another ten minutes or so and you'll be golden."

Jesse wasn't really in the mood to see Charlotte take off down the Riverwalk. Tossing the package of hamburger buns to the trainee, Jesse said, "Okay, then, we'll walk. You clowns finish up eating and take everything back to the firehouse. Don't forget to study those handouts before the next session." Turning to Charlotte, he said, "I'll go along as a precautionary measure. In case my outstanding talents only have a temporary effect. It is the chief's baby, after all."

Charlotte shrugged as if to say, "Better safe than sorry," and began rolling the stroller down the path. Jesse caught up with her, enjoying the victory of the moment. They walked along in cautious silence for a few minutes, ensuring that Maria was safely off in dreamland.

"That was amazing," Charlotte whispered after a bit.

"Actually, that was Ben E. King. 'Amazing' is a different tune." The soft laugh his joke pulled from Charlotte was even more satisfying than Maria's dozing. See? He could do the casual friendship thing here. Bradens's warnings weren't necessary. He was just helping a client help a friend, that was all. Besides, he always liked to make people laugh—why not Charlotte, as well?

"The guys at the firehouse said you've done that on calls. Sing to kids, I mean. How do you manage it?"

It was like having someone ask how he breathed. "It wasn't something I really thought about. The first time was my second or third call on the rig—my first real fire. I was scared. You never really lose the fear. You just sort of make peace with it. Anyway, back in the upper bedroom there was a little boy. We're scary looking with all our gear on, so it's always a challenge to get kids to come to us." The memory of that little boy's dread-filled eyes had never left Jesse. At that moment, he would have done anything it took to gain that boy's confidence and pull him to safety. "I saw a poster from a television show on his wall and I just started singing the theme song."

"And he came to you?"

"Well, it was more like he didn't run away. I just kept singing and walking toward him. I didn't think about whether anyone could hear me on the radio, I was so focused on doing anything to keep that kid from ducking back under that bed. When I got close enough, I grabbed him and just kept singing the whole way down the stairs and out the door so he'd stay still and not struggle."

Charlotte smiled. "Jesse, the singing fireman."

Jesse shot her a look. "Please. I've heard every version of that you can think of, and I don't like a single one of them. It works. It keeps kids—and even some adults—calm when calm is the hardest thing to manage. Bradens does it with his eyes. I do it with my voice."

"Clark's eyes?"

"Every firefighter has a particular gift, a talent. Chief Bradens has a way of looking right into your eyes so that you believe whatever he says. You don't question stuff like that when lives are at stake." He caught Charlotte's gaze and held it. "I take my work at GFVFD very seriously. We all do. We put our lives on the line for it."

"I'm sorry." Her voice was soft, and he regretted calling her out for her teasing. "Really."

"It's okay. Just no cracks about it, all right?" He reached out and touched her hand as it rested on the stroller handle. Something not at all casual and not at all like friendship zinged through his fingers when he did. "I think I've knocked her out cold, poor thing."

Charlotte looked up at him for far longer than was necessary. "You're my hero."

If you choose to go after her, I'd want to know you really mean it.... I don't want the department's most confirmed bachelor to stomp on the heart of my wife's best friend. The chief's warning echoed sensibly in Jesse's brain. Trouble was, the rest of him was busy losing the battle to Charlotte's big brown eyes.

Chapter Eight

Jesse stood in the doorway of Chief Bradens's office Monday morning. "You wanted to see me, Chief?"

"I did. Come on in."

Jesse crossed the room to take the guest chair in front of the chief's desk. "What's up?"

"First off, it seems I owe you some thanks for serenading my daughter the other night." Clark shook his head. "Man, that sounds odd to say."

Jesse made a serious face. "I'm not taking your daughter to the prom, sir."

Clark laughed. "Not on your life, even if she was eighteen years older."

"At least twenty-two years older, boss. And not even then." That was true. If Chief were older—and Bradens was one of the youngest fire chiefs in the state—and his daughter was anything close to Jesse's age, Jesse still wouldn't touch that with a ten-foot pole.

"Okay, well, thanks are in order anyway. It was a pretty nice thing to come home to a sleeping baby. Melba was sure Maria would give Charlotte a load of trouble, and it seems you kept that from happening. The probies were calling you 'the baby whisperer.' It's pretty funny, actually. I think they wonder if you have superpowers or something."

"Feed those boys a decent burger and they'll believe anything," Jesse joked.

"Anyway, I wanted to know if you've given any more thought to the talent-show thing or the inspector's training."

Bradens was not usually one to push on stuff like this—Jesse was beginning to feel the pinch of his predicament. Didn't singing the man's daughter to sleep gain him a "cease-fire" on the church invitations? At least he wasn't riding Jesse for spending an hour walking around the Riverwalk with Charlotte. That hadn't been such a smart idea—that woman had begun to really get under his skin. He'd spent the next hour in the firehouse weight room burning off energy and listing all the reasons to keep clear of the pretty client.

"Yeah, look, I don't know."

The chief leaned in. "I'd take it as a personal favor if you'd emcee the show for us."

Chief's attempts to drag Jesse over the GFCC threshold were getting less subtle every time. It was bad enough when Melba had joined the choir a few months ago, and Bradens went on about fun and fellowship—which Jesse found ironic, because everyone knew the chief couldn't hold a tune if it had a handle tied to it. To Jesse, choir sounded like a bunch of people who barely knew how to have fun standing up singing old songs in silly, shiny robes. Not that he could confirm his theory; the only time he'd darkened the doors of Gordon Falls Community Church had been for Melba's father's funeral a while back, and there had been only community singing in that service.

When Jesse didn't respond, Bradens played his trump

card. "Charlotte was the one who came up with the idea, actually. I'm surprised she didn't mention it to you given the success of your little command performance in the park." That settled it. Charlotte could be relentless. Jesse was sure if he said no to Bradens, Charlotte would just take up the campaign and double it.

"Tell you what. I'll do the talent show if you lay off about the choir."

"Thanks. Think about what I said regarding the inspector, though. Actually, I think you could go further than that. You're a good firefighter, but your real talent is connecting with people. Catching their focus in a crisis. Those are skills I can't really teach. You may think I'm nuts for saying this, but I think if we could rein in that crazy side of yours, you have the makings of a good chief."

Jesse sure wasn't expecting that. "Me? A fire chief?"

"Well, we've got to find some way for you to harness all that charisma for good."

He'd heard some version of that speech—one slightly less complimentary of his personality—regularly from his father. Grow up, settle down, fly straight, take action; it came in a dozen sour flavors. Jesse had really hoped the launching of Sykes Homes would put a damper on that sort of talk. He knew Chief Bradens was demonstrating faith in his abilities; it was just that the topic was a raw nerve. He liked his own plans—even if they had been detoured by the loss of the cottage—and suddenly Bradens was piling new expectations on him. "Thanks for the vote of confidence," was the best answer he could give at the moment, "but like I said, I'm allergic to administration."

"I'm trying to talk the town council into finding the funds to pay for a deputy chief."

Jesse shrugged. Bradens could sweeten the deal all he wanted, but it still didn't really fit in with Jesse's plans for where life was supposed to go from here. He switched to what he hoped was a safer topic. "Speaking of administration, Charlotte will get her occupancy permit this afternoon—we're turning the water back on later today. You'll get your house back." That little benchmark still stung, but the chief had no way of knowing that—only a few of the guys on the crew knew about Jesse's thwarted plans to buy the place. "The place is still rough around the edges but livable. It'll be a beauty, though, when she's done. That woman knows how to make full-blown decorating plans, that's for sure."

"I feel better knowing she's working with you and Mondale rather than some contractor from out of town. She's in a bit of a weird place right now when it comes to that cottage."

At that moment, Jesse saw in Chief Bradens's eyes a glimmer of the niggling suspicion that had bothered him for days. The growing sense that Charlotte might not be thinking with her head right now so much as her heart. "How so?"

"Well, don't you think she's going at this with a little too much—" he searched for the word "—drive?"

Charlotte was indeed going full out on the renovation. It was keeping him busy and swelling his paycheck, but it was also making him a bit worried. "She wouldn't be the first person to take her stress out on the Home Shopping Network, if that's what you're saying." The desire to honor her grandmother and take her mind off her job problems could easily get twisted up in a craving to do things that might not make the most financial sense. "She's taking advantage of the free time in between jobs to give the place the attention it deserves. I can spot the difference."

Could he? He'd accepted her order for premium kitchen fixtures yesterday that were three times as expensive as the ones he'd recommended. While he felt oddly protective of Charlotte, he was also becoming aware that with the right smile, she could make him agree to just about anything. Not that it was his role to rein her in, but hadn't he promised himself to do just that? Let her splurge but splurge wisely? What she'd ordered yesterday couldn't be called a wise splurge by anyone, and yet he hadn't challenged it at all. Charlotte wasn't the only one in a bit of a weird place right now.

"Melba's worried about her." The chief gave a weary sigh. "At the same time, I'd kind of like my house to contain only two females again, if you catch my drift."

"Relax, Chief. Like I said, I should have your guy-to-girl ratio back down to one-to-two by tomorrow." As for what the additional woman would do once she was living in her project and could focus on it full-time… he'd worry about that later.

Charlotte held up Violet Sharpton's latest prayer shawl Wednesday morning with genuine admiration. Karl of Karl's Koffee had fallen and hurt his hip again, and Violet had made him a brown shawl with coffee cups dotting either end, their plumes of steam rising to meet in a swirly pattern down the middle. "Honestly, Violet, if I were still at Monarch, I might ask to put this one—and your flame shawl and the flamingo one—on the cover of a catalogue." Violet had made a fabulous one-of-a-kind prayer shawl, with a flame motif to match his thrill-seeking style, for Max Jones after he'd been hurt in a paralyzing fall. She had exceeded that effort a few months later with one for Max's fiancée, Heather, bearing her favorite birds. A Sharpton Shawl was on its way to becoming a hot Gordon Falls commodity.

"How is the job search going?" Violet asked tenderly. "Seems like there's no loyalty to hardworking people anywhere these days." She handed Charlotte a cup of tea. "I'm just glad the Good Lord sent us another tea drinker." She took back the "Shawlatte," as she'd christened it a minute ago. "It's getting hard to hold my own against the Gordon Falls caffeine junkies." The petite woman's eyes fairly sparkled at her own joke.

"It's still early," Charlotte replied, pasting a smile on her face. "But there have been lots of nibbles, so I'm sure an offer will be here soon." She knew most of the life stories of these women, and none of them had easy lives. Seeing their zest for life despite some whopping challenges gave Charlotte courage. Compared to some of the things these woman had endured—loss of spouses, fires, debilitating diseases, children gone wrong—one layoff seemed barely worthy of complaint.

She did her best to ignore Melba's disbelieving look. The truth was, things weren't going well at all. She'd expected to be choosing between offers by now, not staring into a gaping void of tepid responses to submitted résumés. So much of this loomed out of her control, and it was driving her crazy. She needed action, momentum, anything that felt like results—but the only place she could come close to any of those things was on the cottage renovations. To do that, and do it with excellence, proved such a saving grace. It made her feel successful when success seemed to be edging out of her grasp.

Marge Bowers tugged on Maria's hand as she held the baby. "I saw the sweater your godmother made you, Maria. Your aunt Charlotte knows her stuff." It felt lovely to have her knitting skills receive compliments, especially from these ladies. Maria's biological grandmothers might be gone, but she had a dozen honorary ones here. This morning Charlotte couldn't be certain a fight wasn't going to break out over who got to hold Maria first. "Between Charlotte and your mama, I doubt you'll ever be short of hats or mittens."

"Or scarves," Charlotte added. "Scarves are my favorite."

"I like dishcloths myself," Tina Matthews piped up. "Quick, practical and there are hundreds of designs to choose from."

"Tina gives six as a housewarming gift," Melba related. "I still use my set every day."

"And now I can make you a set, too," Tina said. "Do you know your kitchen color scheme yet?"

Melba started to laugh. "Are you kidding? There are four file boxes, a set of computer files and two scrapbooks on the subject. And that's only the ones I know about."

Charlotte hoped she hadn't been too fast to pull out her smartphone and display an image of the "china-blue and white with yellow accents" color scheme she'd chosen for the kitchen. The resulting *ooh*s and *ahh*s were highly gratifying. The hand-painted porcelain cabinet knobs and handles had arrived the other day, and they were worth every premium penny.

"You've got an eye, Charlotte. Now I know just what color yarn to buy."

The idea that her kitchen sink would someday be graced with both designer weathered copper fixtures *and* a set of handmade color-coordinated dishcloths settled a warm hum in Charlotte's chest. She wasn't quite sure when it had happened, but Gordon Falls was starting to feel like home. Whole days would go by where she didn't even think of Monarch or her city apartment. That made it easier to stomach how she wasn't shuttling back and forth between multiple interviews right now.

"However long you stay, we are glad to have you," Abby Reed replied. "Gordon Falls was starting to feel a little gray-haired before Melba came along."

"And JJ, Alex and Max," Melba added.

"My two cousins have done all right for themselves here," Charlotte admitted, turning her knitting to start a new row. She hadn't really meant "married off" as her version of "done all right," but the knowing looks some of the ladies passed between them meant they'd clearly made the connection.

"Clever you, meeting the town's most charming bachelor fireman your first day in the cottage," Marge teased.

Charlotte rolled her eyes. "Oh, you wouldn't think it was so clever if you saw my kitchen filled with smoke."

"It brought Jesse Sykes to your doorstep." Vi chuckled. "Handsome and handy, that one." For a widow in her seventies, Violet had more energy than anyone else in the room. And more nerve.

"Violet, you really are a piece of work," Jeannie Owens chastised, then broke into a smile. "I hope I grow up to be just like you."

The group erupted in laughter. "Why go for home repair when you could shoot for a man who knows his way around the kitchen?" Marge said in a loud whisper. "I've seen the way Karl looks at you. He already gives you free pie. Wait until he gets that shawl—you'll be eating free for a year!"

Violet snorted her disagreement. "Nonsense. Karl

comps anybody who has to move for Hot Wheels, you know that."

Charlotte's cousin Max, who had received his knitted "FlameThrow" when a climbing accident confined him to a wheelchair, could fit at only one table in Karl's Koffee. It was common knowledge that when someone had to shift seats to make way for Max "Hot Wheels" Jones, Karl gave them free coffee. "I know we all get coffee," Marge countered, wagging her finger, "but you're the only one I know who gets pie. You're special."

Violet, usually never at a loss for a good comeback, didn't reply. She scowled at Marge, but Charlotte was pretty sure the pink in her cheeks wasn't from anger. Anyone who thought Gordon Falls was a quiet, quaint little tourist town on the river where nothing ever happened would get a surprise if they met with this group. The ladies had always been pleasant acquaintances, but they were becoming fast friends. This group had scooped up Melba when she'd come to Gordon Falls in the throes of her father's progressing disease, and now it felt as if they had scooped up Charlotte, as well.

Abby, who had offered to talk retail yarn over lunch after today's knitting session, spoke up. "You know, you could do lots of your job from just about anywhere, couldn't you? You could work for a company in France right from your home."

"If I spoke French," Charlotte admitted. "I have done international work for Monarch, and for my job before that. I used to travel quite a bit, actually. Now that's not so necessary with all the digital communication."

"There was a woman in the shop the other day buying yarn for her grandchildren. She had their video up on her phone and was holding up yarn so they could pick colors right there in front of her. And they were in

New Jersey!" Abby picked up Maria, who had started to fuss a bit in her carrier. "I don't really know how all that stuff works, but it was fun to watch."

"I text my grandchildren all the time," Violet said. "I know stuff that would curl their mother's hair, but I'm keeping my mouth shut. I want them to think they can come to me if they're afraid to talk to Donald and his wife."

"You really are the coolest grandmother ever," Melba said. "I hope you'll be texting Maria when she's in middle school and hates me."

Melba's mother had been gone for years, but Charlotte recognized the still-constant loss that pressed on her own heart. How many times had she picked up her phone to send a photo or text to Mima, only to realize she was gone? It felt as if the huge hole in her life still had ragged, painful edges. Until she had a family of her own, Charlotte vowed to be the kind of support to Maria that Violet was to her grandkids. *I want to trust you'll find me a job, Lord. I want the panic to go away. Until it does, thank You for this amazing circle of women.*

She felt fresh tears sting her eyes until Tina thrust a ball of yarn into her view. "Charlotte, what on earth did I do wrong here? It looks like tumbleweeds."

Charlotte held out her hands. "Let me look at it. I'll have it straightened out in no time." Here, at least, was one thing she knew she could fix, one problem she knew she could solve.

Chapter Nine

Jesse put down his wrench and turned the knob on Charlotte's gorgeous new kitchen faucet. "Drumroll, please."

Charlotte laughed and drummed her hands on the counter. "Ready."

The pipes under the faucet made a host of disturbing noises from behind their cabinet doors. Then, after a few tentative spurts and a gurgle or two, water cascaded from the graceful copper fixture. "Hot and cold running water for Miss Charlotte Taylor, thank you very much," Jesse boasted. "You can move in."

Charlotte was thrilled. This last renovation made the house officially livable. She'd spend her first night in the cottage tonight, even though it meant sleeping on the mattress on the floor, since she hadn't taken delivery yet on the majestic four-poster bed she'd found at the local antiques store. While waiting on some of the final utilities—and a disturbingly empty e-mail inbox—Charlotte had poured over catalogues, invaded furniture stores and even scoured local flea markets in search of perfect finds. Even Jesse had remarked that the place managed to boast a surprising amount of furniture already. It was much better to focus on the decorating progress she *could* control than to ruminate on the employment process she could not. A dozen curtains came in, but the two dozen résumés she'd most recently sent out hadn't produced any response.

She poked her head into a cabinet to produce a brand-new stovetop kettle and two mugs. "Shall we celebrate? Without the smoke signals this time?"

Jesse pulled a rag from his toolbox and wiped the worst of the grime from his hands. He had a royal-blue T-shirt on today that did distracting things to his eyes. "Tea?"

"Yogurt doesn't feel very festive, and that's all I've got in the fridge right now. I was heading out for groceries this afternoon."

"Well, if it's either tea or yogurt, I'll opt for tea. As long as it's really strong." He clearly had no interest in the brew and was consenting for her benefit. Charlotte hadn't seen that level of consideration in a guy for a long time. How nice that he sensed what an important moment this was for her, how it was much more than two mugs of tea on a flea-market table—it was a declaration of resilience. Jesse held up one finger. "Go ahead and put the kettle on…I'll be right back."

Turning the brand-new faucet lever warmed her all the way out to her fingertips. The perfection of it felt like the best antidote to the sagging job search—satisfying and empowering. This house had been waiting for her. Okay, the first welcome hadn't gone well, but despite that kitchen fire she knew the house loved her.

That was silly of course; a house was incapable of loving her. Still, how many times had she felt her knitting comfort her—or mock her when things went horribly wrong? Charlotte drew strongly from her surroundings; her tactile world had always affected her deeply. The scent of her favorite tea filling this kitchen would feel like an anointing; a blessing of her life here. A promise that it would all work out in the end. Not that she could or would explain such a thing to the likes of Jesse Sykes.

The porch door slammed as she was placing the tea cozy—one she'd knitted herself—around the steeping pot, and Jesse entered the room with a small handful of flowers and a package of cookies. "What's a tea party without cookies?" He waved the package and the flowers at her. "Although they've been in the backseat of my truck for a week—we may be looking at more crumbs than cookies."

Charlotte didn't think her smile could get any wider. He'd understood her need to celebrate. And yet his gesture wasn't forced or overwhelming; it was just an honest gift of what he could scramble together. "Are those from Mrs. Hawthorne's yard?" She didn't know her new next-door neighbor well enough to judge how much of a trespass Jesse had just committed.

Jesse made a "who me?" face. "Could be. Could be I just happened to have black-eyed susans in my glove box. Or a flat of flowers in the back of my truck. You'd have no way of knowing. You're completely innocent."

The closest thing Charlotte had to a vase was a tall blue glass canning jar, which she filled with water and set in the center of the table. She grabbed a small tin tray from a box in the hallway, laid a paper towel across it and arranged the rather sad assortment of broken cookies on the towel. The tea, flowers, mugs and cookies made a comical vignette, and he couldn't help but laugh as she placed a few restaurant packets of sugar by the teapot. "One lump or two?"

"With only a brother in the house growing up, I'm not exactly up on my tea party etiquette." He pulled the chair out for Charlotte with a dramatic gesture, then made a show of easing himself into the opposite chair. He winced a little when it creaked a bit under his weight, looking like the proverbial bull in the china shop of her furnishings. "What am I supposed to do?"

Charlotte laughed. "Drink tea and eat cookies—or what's left of the cookies. This isn't a test." She poured his cup, then her own. "This is a chai tea—it's strong like coffee, so you might actually like it."

Jesse smelled the aroma wafting up from the mug, his face scrunching in suspicion. "Doubtful. Might be good for dunking, though." He caught her eye. "I am allowed to dunk, aren't I?"

"I heartily encourage the dunking of cookies. I'm a dunker myself, you know." After a second, she felt compelled to add, "Thanks."

"For putting in your sink?" His eyes told her he knew exactly why she had thanked him, and that it had nothing to do with the sink.

"No." The word slid soft and warm between them. The aroma of chai tea in her new kitchen settled around her like a consecration, with all the comfort of a fluffy shawl on a cold evening.

Jesse added two sugars before even tasting the tea, then lifted the mug to his lips. "Um—" he paused, clearly looking for the right description "—delicious?"

"You hate it." Charlotte found she wasn't offended at all. In fact, she was more enchanted by his efforts to hide it. "No, really, it's okay."

"I'm a coffee guy," he explained, spreading his hands in admission.

"I like coffee, too," she said, then wondered why she

was trying to build connections with him. "I just don't have any in the cottage right now. I'll get some this afternoon." Why had she said that? Why was she extending social invitations to a guy she'd already decided wasn't a good match, even if she was looking for someone? "So you can have coffee while you work and all."

Plausible as the excuse was, they both knew that wasn't what she'd meant. Things were tumbling in a direction Charlotte didn't really understand or endorse. Only she knew she didn't want Jesse to leave—now or even soon. She told herself it was that she wasn't ready to be in the house all alone, but that rang as false as Jesse's compliment of her chai tea.

"So your Mima wasn't a tea drinker? Even with all the china cups and all?"

Why was it that every time Charlotte talked herself into dismissing the tug she felt toward Jesse, he'd say something that pulled her to him again? She needed to talk about Mima. A lot. Charlotte didn't like how it felt as if Mima were slipping from her memory, as if she had to speak aloud to secure all those wonderful memories in her life now that Mima was gone. It was silly—she'd never even spoken that often to Mima. Their communication in the last few years was mostly fun texts or postcards or jots of short correspondence. Why the burning need to keep talking about her? Grief did funny things to a person.

Charlotte wrapped her hands around the warmth of her mug—despite the June afternoon heat—and wished for the dozens of china plates, cups and saucers to be surrounding her here in the cottage kitchen instead of still back in Chicago. "Mima drank tea, coffee, cocoa, anything. She was always bringing exotic blends of coffee and tea home to me. And that spicy Mexican hot chocolate. She loved that, too. When I was little, she would make me tea or coffee in my own special cup that she kept at her house just for me. A real china cup, not a plastic kiddie thing. Of course, the drink was more milk than coffee or tea, and it was loaded with sugar, but I felt so grown up when I drank it." Tears clamped her throat again. "Important, you know? She was great at making me feel like I meant the world to her."

"That's nice. A rare thing." There was a shadow in Jesse's eyes as he looked at her. A dark place behind all the sympathy. After a second or two, Charlotte realized it was envy. Hunger, even. It made her wonder if Jesse had ever had anyone in his life to make him feel important. Was that where the showmanship personality and the hero-rescuer drive came from? She'd had so much affirmation in her life, it stung to see the lack of it played out so clearly in his features.

Even though she knew it might not be a safe question, she asked anyway. "Anyone like that in your life?"

Is there anyone like that in my life?

Jesse swallowed hard. Charlotte had asked the million-dollar question, and he found himself unable to dredge up one of his smart-aleck evasive answers. Not here, not when he was faced with the collection of sweet memories playing across her face. To be so loved—it must be amazing. And then again gut-wrenching to have that love taken away. She had on a peach-colored tunic, and he watched her finger the simple gold cross that sat in the V neckline of the top. He knew, without having to ask, that it had been her grandmother's. He realized he'd never seen her without it, and that she touched it whenever she talked about Mima. He could guess that she'd put it on the day the beloved old woman had died and she hadn't taken it off since.

To love someone so hard and know they loved you just as much—that hadn't ever really been the case in his family. Sure, he'd mourn his parents when they were gone, but it wouldn't be like the loss he could see in Charlotte's eyes when she talked about this amazing grandmother of hers.

"Not like that." It seemed the safest way to answer her question. His memories of his grandparents were mostly about instructions and expectations. He and Randy got along, but they'd never been particularly close. His mom loved him—in a safe, mom kind of way—but not with the fierce, lasting affection Charlotte seemed to have known. And Dad? Well, he supposed Dad thought the pushy way he treated Jesse was what parental love was supposed to look like.

"I'm sorry." Charlotte looked at him—really looked at him, as though she could see all the regrettable things going through his head. No judgment, just awareness. A sad sort of understanding that wandered a little too close to pity.

Guilt twisted Jesse's gut. "Don't get me wrong, my parents love me and all, but they don't really—" he couldn't find a word that didn't sound ungrateful and even petulant "—root for me." He pushed out a sigh and took another swig of the tolerable tea just to buy time to think. "I have a younger brother, and he does all the expected stuff. All the right, successful things moms and dads think their kids ought to do when they grow up. Great job, big house, all the trimmings. They say they don't compare, but…" He found he didn't want to finish that sentence.

"You save people." She said it with something close

to awe. The wideness of her eyes pulled at him. He was wrong; it wasn't pity he saw in her features—it was "you deserve so much more." It wasn't fair what that did to him. He wasn't prepared for how she got to him without even realizing what she was doing.

"Yeah, I think that confuses them most of all. The whole volunteer firefighter thing makes no sense to them. Why risk myself for nothing? At least that's how they see it. Mom never comes out and says it like that, but Dad never minces words on the subject."

Charlotte picked up a broken cookie. "Your dad doesn't like you in the volunteer fire department?"

"He thinks of it as a waste of time. Or close to that— I don't think he's been quite that harsh. More like an unnecessary distraction that seems to be keeping me from reaching my professional potential." Jesse picked up a piece of cookie and dunked it in the mug. "He'd be happier if I were more successful."

"More like your brother?"

"If you mean my brother whose marriage just fell apart and who is working on his second ulcer, then you can see why maybe I don't share the old man's opinion." Jesse hadn't meant the words to come out with quite that much edge, but Charlotte had hit a nerve. "I have my own idea of success. I have big plans for a remodeling business." He stopped himself there, afraid that if he launched into those plans he might reveal how he'd wanted this cottage as his first project. Right now he didn't want Charlotte to know that. It would make everything weird, and it was weird enough already.

"You're different than him."

The simple words struck a completely separate nerve. The hungry nerve, the unfed craving. She managed to meet some need in him he wasn't even aware of until she'd waltzed into Gordon Falls and stymied his plans. How had she managed to articulate the one thing, the one thought, that he could never seem to get his parents to understand? "Completely." He didn't trust himself to go any further than that.

"I don't think I'd like this brother of yours very much." She'd said it casually, before either of them realized the natural progression of that thought. It unwound itself in Jesse's brain like a mathematical equation: *if C dislikes R and J is the opposite of R, therefore C must like J.* She knew it, too, for suddenly she stared too hard at her cookie instead of looking at him.

He had to find some way out of this too-close moment. "You'd hate his cooking."

"Most guys can't cook their way out of a paper bag." Charlotte was trying, as he'd done, to lighten the moment, but it wasn't working for either of them. "Well, evidently, except for chefs, and you and your burgers."

Ah, now she'd done it. Had she knowingly thrown that door open, or just by accident? He puffed up his chest. "I am an outstanding cook. I could probably cook circles around half the restaurants in Gordon Falls, and not just on firehouse fare. I'll have you know my skills extend far beyond chili and burgers."

Her eyes narrowed at his boasting. "Do they? So not only can you install ovens, but you can use one, too?"

There was just enough tease in her words to seal her fate. "I'm on duty tomorrow night, but Friday you are going to find out just how well this man can cook his way out of a paper bag. As a matter of fact, I could probably cook a paper bag and you'd think it was delicious." Before Charlotte could put in one word of protest, Jesse stood up and began opening the mostly empty cupboards and fridge, taking stock of what was here and what he'd need to bring. "You said you were going to the grocery store and back to Chicago for a load of stuff tomorrow, right?"

"Yes?" She looked as if she had just opened Pandora's box and wasn't sure if she should start regretting it.

"You're coming back Friday? You've got a saucepan?" He circled his hands to mimic a deep round pan just in case she didn't know her way around a kitchen.

"I'll be back Friday. And of course I have a saucepan." Her hands crossed over her chest.

"Frying pan?"

"Yes. Two, in fact."

He scratched his chin, the meal planning itself in his head already. "Bring both." Grabbing a receipt from off the counter, he started writing. Within five minutes he'd given her a list of items and suggested tableware. This was going to be fun. If there was anything Jesse Sykes knew how to do as well as build things, it was cook things. Delicious, incredible things. Friends cooked for friends all the time, right? It wasn't a date. Not even close.

Charlotte sat there, running her hand down the list with her mouth open. "Um, I've got everything on here but a cheese grater."

"I'll bring mine. And my spices. I don't trust the grocery store stuff most people get—no offense, but it makes all the difference. Can you be back in Gordon Falls by five-thirty?"

She shrugged. "Works for me."

Charlotte's smile held the tiny hint of "you gotta be kidding me" that touched the edges of her eyes. It kindled an insane need to put that doubt to rest and flat-out amaze her. Jesse knew—down to his boots knew—that he could. He just wasn't going to take the time to analyze why.

Chapter Ten

Charlotte pulled open her back door Friday night to the sight of Jesse holding a pair of stuffed grocery bags. A bouquet of flowers tottered on the top of one bag while a loaf of delicious-smelling bread poked out of the other. He grinned. "Hungry?"

She grabbed one of the bags and held the door open. A whiff of "clean guy"—that extraordinary mix of soap and man and a hint of whatever it was he put on his hair—wafted by as he passed, and Charlotte felt her stomach flip. Maybe she should have stayed in Chicago and said no to this little feast. That probably would have been the smart thing to do, but this didn't really feel like a date, and besides, Jesse didn't strike her as the kind of guy who took no for an answer.

Still, there was no denying the guy was seriously attractive. And toting incredible food. God must have known what He was doing when He ensured she wouldn't be hosting Jesse alone.

Just as he put the bag down on the counter, Jesse caught site of Charlotte's new housemate. His entire face changed.

"You have a cat."

Jesse said the words slowly, biting off the end of the last word with a sharp *t*. This was clearly not a welcome revelation.

"I do." She forced ignorant cheer into her voice. For the fifth time today, Charlotte wondered if Melba had known *exactly* what she was doing when she'd presented her with the furry little wonder when Charlotte got back from Chicago this afternoon. She walked over to the kitchen seat where her new companion sat staring suspiciously at her guest cook. "Jesse, meet Mo."

Mo curled up the end of his tail in something Charlotte hoped did not translate to "I was here first."

"Hello, Mo." Charlotte could practically watch Jesse's back straighten. Dinner was in danger of becoming a territorial battle, and the man had been here all of thirty seconds.

"You brought a cat into a house under renovation." Charlotte could practically hear Jesse's brain trying to link the two ideas. While he never said it, and was trying hard not to look it, the man's every pore seemed to seep "Are you out of your mind?" She watched him mentally sift through potential verbal responses before he settled on "That will make things interesting." Then he set down the bag of groceries they'd both forgotten he was holding.

Charlotte, who'd already set down the bag with the bread, walked over and stroked Mo. He arched his back up to meet her hand, keeping one yellow eye on Jesse as if to say "See? She likes me." "Melba gave him to me as an early birthday present. She has a cat she loves very much."

"I remember." They weren't happy memories, that much was clear. He chose his next words carefully. "I'm surprised Melba failed to remember that working on the house with Pinocchio didn't go especially well."

Mo apparently took offense to that, leaping in a brown, black and white streak toward what would be the dining room. Evidently he wasn't going to stand around and listen to Jesse defame his character. She imagined he'd head up to the bedroom soon, as the mattress on the floor had become his favorite spot since this afternoon. "She mentioned it might be a bit of a bumpy ride at first. But I love Pinocchio, and he was great company curled up next to me in the guest room at Melba's. Mo's been fine and settling in all day. It'll be nice to have company. You told me you were a dog person, but I didn't realize that meant you were an anti-cat person."

Jesse began taking items out of the bag. "I'm not an anti-cat guy. I just recognize that construction can stress animals out. You may be in for a bumpier ride than Melba let on." She watched him choose to get past it, pushing out a breath and turning to her with the bouquet of flowers from the grocery bag. "These are for you. Paid for, fair and square."

She didn't want to let Mo ruin the evening, either. She'd considered Mo a convenient excuse, a way to cut the evening short if things felt as if they were getting too close. Now, looking at him all spiffed up and offering a bouquet of flowers, Charlotte realized she liked Jesse. She *really* liked him. And that could still be okay; one dinner with him didn't constitute a lifetime of sirens and anxious nights. It was just a friendly dinner. She didn't have to stress over it the way she might have over a *real* date.

She took the flowers, delighted that he'd chosen a mixture of wildflowers and sunny pastels rather than something serious like roses or ordinary like carnations. The arrangement fit the room, fit the sturdy little table that would host their meal. "Thank you. They're lovely. I brought a vase from my Chicago apartment, too. I was going to put some greenery from the backyard in it, but this is much nicer." She reached into a box on another counter, found a doily Mima had crocheted and set it on the table with the vase right in the center.

They worked together on the meal as easily as they had worked on the bathtub. Jesse was masterful in the kitchen, doling out small jobs like chopping shallots while hovering over four different pans of delectable-smelling food. It made the cottage feel like a true home. A meal with friends.

Only it didn't seem to want to stay just "a meal with friends." Jesse would catch her eye every now and then, smiling confidently as he explained why this had to boil for just a minute more, or why that ingredient had to be added just a little at a time, and her pulse would catch just a bit. He sang snippets of Sam Cooke's "You Send Me" while he worked, and his voice swirled around her as it filled the kitchen. Then he lifted the lid on one saucepan and spooned up a creamy white sauce that smelled delicious. Jesse tasted it, eyes closed in assessment, added a little more of something, then tasted again. His resulting smile beamed of victory. "Here, try this." He held out a spoon, and Charlotte couldn't have refused for all the world.

Had someone told him Alfredo sauce was her favorite? Had he run into Melba or Clark at the grocery store? Or was this just another way Jesse Sykes knew how to keep his customer happy? "Oh," she said, going beyond just a taste to lick the spoon completely clean. "Oh, my. Wow."

"My family may be Anglo, but Italian is my specialty. Douse that handmade fresh spinach fettuccine with this, add the Brussels sprouts I've got going over there, and you'll think you've died and gone to heaven."

Charlotte winced. "I'm…um…not really a fan of Brussels sprouts." Actually, she didn't know anyone who was a fan of Brussels sprouts.

"You haven't tasted mine." He said it as if resistance to his particular brand of vegetable would be impossible. The tone of his voice made her believe him. Or at least want to believe him. "Close your eyes."

She gave him a look. "A bit dramatic, don't you think?"

He gave her a look right back. "You'll eat those words right after you eat my Brussels sprouts."

Parking a hand on one hip, Charlotte countered, "You know that sounds ridiculous, don't you?"

Jesse wagged his fingers in front of her face until she rolled her eyes before squinting them shut. She heard him fiddle with the top of a saucepan, then the sound of his voice very close and soft. "Open." He sang the word more than said it, his tone smooth and coaxing. She felt him close with her eyes closed, smelled the soap on his skin now mixed with the marvelous scents of his cooking. Maybe Brussels sprouts had been given a bad rap. She felt the fork against her tongue and bit down on what he offered.

Oh.

Brussels sprouts were the epitome of gross vegetables, the thing universally turning up child and adult noses everywhere. These could not have been Brussels sprouts. They were crunchy and a bit crispy, with something savory hiding between the tiny green leaves. Half a dozen different tastes and textures mixed on her tongue. This was the chocolate cake of vegetables. It

2 FREE BOOKS

ABSOLUTELY FREE · GUARANTEED

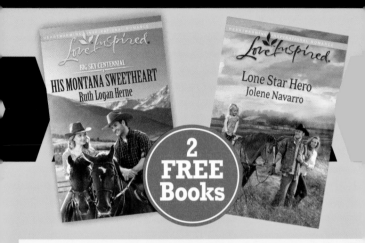

Love Inspired

BIG SKY CENTENNIAL

HIS MONTANA SWEETHEART
Ruth Logan Herne

Love Inspired

Lone Star Hero
Jolene Navarro

2 FREE Books

We'd like to send you another 2 excellent reads from the series you're enjoying now **ABSOLUTELY FREE** to say thank you for choosing to read one of our fine books, and to give you a real taste of just how much fun the Harlequin™ reader service really is. There's no catch, and you're under no obligation to buy anything — EVER! Claim your 2 FREE Books today.

Plus you'll get 2 FREE Mystery Gifts (worth about $10)!

Pam Powers
for Harlequin Reader Service

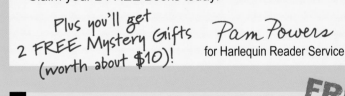

FRE

VALUE:	COMBINED BOOK COVER PRICE:	POSTAGE DUE:
	Over $10 (US)/Over $10 (CAN)	$0

COMPLETE YOUR POSTCARD AND RETURN IT TODAY

Plus 2 FREE Mystery Gifts!

2 FREE BOOKS

ABSOLUTELY FREE · GUARANTEED

CLAIM YOUR FREE GIFTS

YES! Please send me my **2 FREE BOOKS** and **2 FREE GIFTS.** I understand that, as explained on the back of this card, I am under no obligation to purchase anything!

2 FREE Books

Affix sticker here

M-88D1-0792-MG

❏ I prefer the regular-print edition
105/305 IDL GF9X

❏ I prefer the larger-print edition
122/322 IDL GF9X

FIRST NAME

LAST NAME

ADDRESS

APT.#

CITY

STATE/PROV.

ZIP/POSTAL CODE

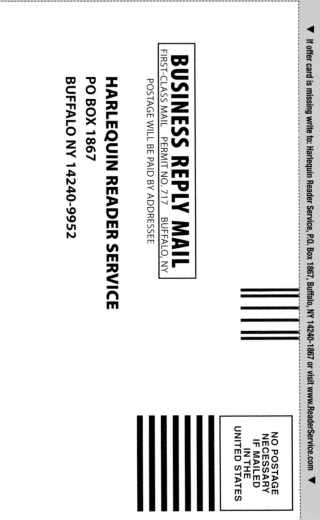

BUSINESS REPLY MAIL
FIRST-CLASS MAIL   PERMIT NO. 717   BUFFALO, NY

POSTAGE WILL BE PAID BY ADDRESSEE

HARLEQUIN READER SERVICE
PO BOX 1867
BUFFALO NY 14240-9952

NO POSTAGE
NECESSARY
IF MAILED
IN THE
UNITED STATES

couldn't be those nasty green orbs everyone avoided in the produce aisle. He was tricking her; he had to be.

Charlotte opened her eyes wide, unprepared for the closeness of Jesse's triumphant face. There was a second piece on the fork, which she immediately ate. "Wow," she said with her mouth full. He was so close, so dauntingly handsome, and he had just fed her his cooking. At this very moment, Jesse Sykes was the most attractive man on earth. Denying it was just plain impossible. "That's a vegetable?" she whispered, just for something to say because his nearness was fogging her thinking.

"You should see what I do with butternut squash," he boasted, "but this is a personal specialty." He reached out and brushed a bit of sauce or butter or whatever that splendid concoction was off her chin. She shivered at his touch, fighting off the dizzying sensation his brown eyes kindled in the pit of her stomach.

Talk. Talk before you do something else, something you don't want to do right now. "Every Brussels sprout on earth should stand up and thank you." She hated how flustered she sounded, hated how he knew exactly how he'd wowed her and was currently reveling in it. "I hope you made a lot of those." She ducked out of the dazzle of his eyes to peer into the covered pan.

"Pace yourself. You'll want to save room for dessert."

The man had made dessert. That was just plain fighting dirty. If this man produced a cheesecake then all hopes of sensibility were lost. Charlotte puttered around the kitchen, fighting the sinking feeling that was like drowning but a whole lot sweeter.

Jesse stood still, watching her, as in control of the moment as she was out of it. "You want to slice up some lemon for the water?" The words were mundane enough, but his eyes seemed to say "So I don't kiss you right now up against the refrigerator?"

There was a journal page upstairs in Charlotte's bedroom listing all the reasons why dating a firefighter was a bad idea. Right now Charlotte couldn't remember a single one of them.

Jesse had eaten in some pretty spectacular restaurants, had even done the firehouse's entire Thanksgiving dinner last year, but no meal had ever filled him with the satisfaction of Charlotte's little table currently spread with his cooking. Even Mo—the predatory little beast—had come in from the living room to view the spectacle, perhaps hoping to leverage his cuteness into a little creamy Alfredo sauce.

Jesse gave him a "my turn" glare as he walked over to pull out Charlotte's chair for her. The urge to run a hand through the cascade of her blond hair caught him up short, and he nearly tripped on his way around to his side of the table. His plan to keep the evening light and friendly was falling prey to the look of utter delight on her face. It sank deep into his chest and settled there like a craving. She took such a rich pleasure in the world, in small things, in things he often took for granted. What gave her such a rare capacity for joy like that? Even in the face of all the obstacles life had thrown at her recently?

He settled himself in his chair and reached for the serving spoon. "Dig in."

She cocked her head at him. "No grace?"

It took him a minute to realize what she'd said.

"Grace," she repeated. "Over the food."

"Um, sure," he said, fumbling. "Why not."

Charlotte extended her hand for his. Jesse was sure

a man ought not to feel the sparks her hand left in his palm while saying prayers. He told himself not to luxuriate in the softness of her hands while he closed his eyes. He'd never been the hand-holding kind of guy, but right now holding her hands felt to him like whatever he saw shoot through her eyes when she tasted his cooking.

"Thank You, Father, for this wonderful meal Jesse has set before us."

Jesse wasn't prepared for her words. He was expecting some rote little poem, some Sunday school verse said in memorized monotone. Charlotte was praying. Real, actual, as-if-she-talked-to-God-every-day conversation. Over his food. "I'm grateful for this house, for all You've made possible, for all the work that went into this delicious food. I am, quite surprisingly, thankful for Brussels sprouts, too. Who'd have thought?"

Jesse opened one eye to see her smiling, eyes closed as she carried on the easy dialogue. He'd not seen grace—or even prayer—ever look like this. It startled him, shaking something loose that felt as if it didn't belong rattling around under his ribs.

"Bless the hands that prepared this food," Charlotte tightened her grip on Jesse's hand, making his pulse gallop for a moment, "and may it nourish our bodies. In Your Son's name, Amen."

"Amen," Jesse gulped out, hoping that was the right thing to say. He was still trying to work out what had just happened. Chief Bradens had been known to say a formal grace over meals at the firehouse, but they never sounded like that, and they never made him feel as though someone had just hit him with a thousand-watt floodlight, dazzled and blinking for focus.

"This looks incredible. I want to stuff myself silly—

I've tasted all of it and I think you're about to meet my piggish side."

"Knock yourself out." He wanted to see her piggish side. He wanted to see her unrestrained enjoyment, to hear her groan with delight and lick the sauce off her fingers and ask for seconds if not thirds. He'd enjoyed lots of compliments on his food before, but those mostly fed his ego. Her pleasure in his cooking only made him want to make her happier. That wasn't the kind of selfless gratification Jesse was used to, and he didn't know how to deal with the feeling. He only knew he liked it, and he wanted more of it.

He ate with enthusiasm. He watched her eat with relish, going on about this project and that fixture between raves over the food and sighs of what could only be termed gastronomic infatuation. The combination of Charlotte gushing over his food and espousing big renovation dreams was like catnip to Jesse—to put it in Mo's terms. His insides were buzzing like live wires, sparking with every small touch, every adorable look. More than once he yearned to kiss the Alfredo sauce off her cheek, off her lips, no matter how stridently Chief Bradens and his own sense of caution had warned him off. He had found women disarmingly attractive before, but this was a whole new scale of allure.

"I think I should go ahead and get the custom ironwork for the front steps. I just don't see anything I like as much in the catalogues. I love the idea about Mima's quilt motif worked into the front railings." He could see it as clearly as she could. The price tag started not to matter. There was something about being near her, as if she gave off some kind of magnetism he was helpless to resist. "Irresistible" suddenly wasn't a clichéd description—he found Charlotte wholly, genuinely irresistible. This was becoming dangerous on any number of fronts.

By the time he made coffee and doled out French vanilla ice cream to start melting all over the berry cobbler he'd pulled out of the oven for dessert, Jesse felt his personal and professional warning system completely short-circuit. She was talking about imported glass tile backsplashes and granite countertops while she tore off a piece of bread and mopped up the last bit of sauce off her plate. He knew just the color stone that would set off her eyes, and it no longer mattered that it was the most expensive. She was Charlotte. The world would line up to do her bidding because at that moment, he would have said yes to anything she asked. Even the dumb cat. She had him hooked. What made him most nervous of all was that he could already feel the ache that would start when he walked out this door tonight and never let up until he was near her again.

It scared him to death. He knew he was on the verge of a terrifying loss of control he wouldn't have predicted and couldn't contain. Jesse knew guys who got this way about fire—it drew them, fascinated them, nearly possessed them in a way that made them fearless. *It's also what gets them hurt or killed,* he reminded himself. When emotion overpowered thought, damage happened. The very thing he'd hoped to give Charlotte in this project—an objective eye, a grounded opinion as to what was a worthwhile splurge and what was reckless spending—was about to go out the window. This was not good.

Jesse turned back from returning the ice cream to the freezer and found her already digging into the cobbler right there at the counter—she hadn't even waited for him to set them down at the table. She had a spot of purple right at the corner of her mouth, and she let out this intoxicating little hum as she found it with the tip of her tongue.

That was it. Without a thought to the consequences, without even wondering if she'd welcome the advance, because every cell in his body already told him she would, Jesse kissed her.

The taste of his cooking on her lips was enthralling. When her initial surprise melted into surrender, he lost the ability to think straight. But when Charlotte began to return his kiss? That put him over the edge. Who cared what Bradens thought? It was one night, one dinner, one kiss. One really amazing kiss.

"Jesse…" She gasped his name, falling back against the counter as if the house had shifted off its foundations. He felt the same way, as if the world was whirling around him, spiraling out from the place where her hand still lay on his chest.

He put his hand atop hers, wondering if she could feel the pounding. "I…um…" He knew he should say something smooth, something casual and clever, but he came up empty. She'd undone him with one kiss, frightening as it was. He craved another kiss so much that he feared being able to control himself if he took one.

Not good, Sykes, not good at all.

Chapter Eleven

Crash. The moment came to a loud halt when a dish clattered to the floor. Mo had, at some point, leaped up onto the countertop in an effort to get at the melted ice cream and had succeeded in knocking over the cobbler dish. The cat screeched and bolted back into the dark of the living room. They both looked down to see white cream and purple cobbler splattered all over the floor and Charlotte's light-colored pants.

Charlotte didn't know whether to thank Mo or to kick the furry, meddling feline to the curb. The moment— whatever it was—was gone, replaced with a sticky mess and the casualty of one of her favorite pairs of pants.

Jesse had already grabbed a towel from the counter and was picking the pieces of the plate off the floor, muttering unkind things about cats. She stared at him, wanting to blink and shake her head, needing to know what had just happened and whether or not she should regret it.

It had been a spectacular kiss. The kind that made her sensibilities go white like an old-fashioned flash-bulb, the kind that ought to be the first kiss between soul mates. Only now that the bubble had popped, she could name half a dozen reasons why Jesse Sykes was not the mate of her soul. And as for Jesse himself, if the kiss had affected him the way it had her, it no longer showed.

"See, not too hard to clean up." Jesse slid the broken china into the wastebasket and tossed the purple-blotched towel into the sink. "I don't think you can say the same for those pants." He turned to her, an "oh well" smile in his eyes, as if it had been a simple kitchen mishap. "There's enough dessert to start over."

"I don't think we ought to." She knew she didn't sound at all convinced. She wasn't—confused was closer to accurate.

His disappointment was so appealing. "Really? My cobbler's even better than my Brussels sprouts."

Charlotte leaned against the cabinets. "Jesse…"

He leaned up against the same cabinets, inches from her. "Hey, it's okay." He shrugged. "But it was a really nice kiss."

She shut her eyes for a moment, slipping her hand up to press it to her own lips while she launched a prayer up to heaven for the right words. "I know there's something…here." She opened her eyes again, wanting to make him understand. "The meal, the kiss— you know how to sweep a woman off her feet. It's just that…" How could she make him understand when she wasn't even sure what she wanted at the moment herself?

He put a hand to his chest as if wounded. "I feed you fettuccine Alfredo and you shoot me down? Ouch." His words were harsh but his eyes held that teasing glint she found most irresistible about him.

"I need to take it a whole lot slower than this." That much was true. She still hadn't figured out if, in the space of one meal, Jesse Sykes had truly disintegrated her conviction not to get involved with men in his line of work. Had she truly overcome that fear? Or was it just pushed aside by Jesse's….*Jesseness,* just to return later when her guard was down? "I like being with you," she admitted, "but we have a lot of ground to cover and a bunch of things we have to…I have to work out. Or through. Or something." She let her head fall back against the cabinets. "'It's complicated' sounds so stupid, but it is."

"It doesn't have to be. I don't think this has to be a big, complicated deal. I do know I don't want tonight to end here, like this."

"Maybe it's better that it does. At least for the sake of my pants." *If not my convictions.*

Jesse ran one hand through his hair. "I'll tell you what. Why don't you go upstairs and get those into water or soap—or whatever you do to get blueberry out of something—and I'll clean up here? Then we'll figure out what comes next. No sweeping off of any feet."

It seemed as good a plan as any. She needed fifteen minutes out of the pull of his eyes, away from the way he seemed to fill the room and cloud her thinking. "Okay."

Charlotte dashed upstairs, slipped into a pair of jeans and filled the bathroom sink—the beautiful bathroom sink Jesse had installed three days ago—with cold water and soap. She dunked the stained pants into the sink and scrubbed a few seconds before stopping to stare at herself in the mirror.

What do you want, Charlotte? What do you want to do about that man downstairs in your kitchen?

She knew Jesse. Knew his character and personality as if they'd spent years together instead of weeks. He probably thought she hadn't noticed his reaction to her prayer over the food, but she'd seen it. It was so strong she'd nearly felt it. Still, all that awareness wasn't the same as a man of faith, a man whose soul could match with hers. In all the time they'd spent together they'd only skittered around the topic of church and God. She knew his dreams, but not his values. And quite frankly, it wasn't hard to guess at his reputation where women were concerned.

And then there was the question of firefighting. It wasn't his whole life, as the police force had been for Dad, but it was a big part. Would it always be there, or would his volunteer duties eventually fade as his business grew to take more and more of his time? And was dating your general contractor ever a good idea? The questions seemed to rise up and swallow her clarity the same way the rising bubbles rose up to cover her hands.

Mo wandered into the bathroom, drawn out of his hiding spot in her bedroom by the lights and sounds of her spontaneous load of laundry. Charlotte pulled her hands from the suds and pointed a finger at the cat. "The jury's still out on you, mister."

Mo simply sat down on the tile and wrapped his tail around his legs, a picture of all the calm and patience she currently lacked. If he had any advice or warning, she couldn't decipher it from his eyes. Charlotte would have to work this one out on her own.

She touched the framed photo of Mima as she passed it on the hallway table at the top of the stairs. *What do I do, Mima? Why is this man in my life now when you aren't here to tell me what to do with him?*

Charlotte had enough married friends to know that to come downstairs to a man responsible for a spotless kitchen was a wonder indeed. He had his stuff packed up in the grocery bags but his face told her he wasn't the least bit ready to leave. "Talk to me," he said as he sat down at the table she now noticed was set with two cups of coffee. "Tell me what's whirling around in that pretty head of yours."

She sat down. Talking about this was a good idea, and she was glad for the table between them. She knew he wasn't clouding her thinking on purpose, but that didn't mean he wasn't very good at it. "I'm worried this won't turn out to be such a good idea."

"Because I'm working on your house."

She owed him the further explanation. "That's just part of it." She ran her hands across the thighs of her jeans, wiping the last of the water from the upstairs washing project. "My dad was a policeman."

His face changed, understanding darkening his features. "I didn't know that."

There was a lot he didn't know. That was the whole point. "I've spent a lot of nights watching my mom get eaten alive from the stress of waiting for bad news. I made a promise to myself that I'd never let myself in for that kind of life."

Jesse leaned back in his chair. "You've known I was a firefighter literally from the moment you met me."

"I didn't say I couldn't be *friends* with you." That felt like a weak defense.

"Friends don't kiss like that. But this doesn't have to become superserious overnight, Charlotte. It's not an all-or-nothing proposition."

Charlotte's chest was filled with a mixed-up host of reactions. He'd felt it. Of course he'd felt it—how could he not feel what she felt humming between them? Only Jesse looked so much more in control of the situation than she felt. "Look, I'm kind of an impulsive person."

Was she explaining her choice in backsplash tiles or how she'd kissed him back?

"Really? I hadn't noticed." Did he have to smile like that? All velvety and cavalier?

She struggled forward, telling the flutter in her stomach to behave itself. "It makes it hard to hang on to certain...challenging convictions."

Jesse gave her a look that said he rather enjoyed challenging people's convictions. Right—there was one of the problems with this whole situation. "Okay."

"My faith is really important to me. Maybe more now than it's been at any point in my life. It'd be a bad idea to get serious with someone who couldn't share that with me. I know you don't get that, but—"

"I do get that."

She hadn't expected that response. "You do?"

"I liked your grace. Never heard it done quite that way before. I'm okay with it."

"I'm glad to hear that, but it goes a bit deeper for me than table grace. There are—"

He cut her off. "Do you know I said yes to emceeing the talent show at your church tomorrow night? I figured maybe it was time I stopped ditching that stuff."

Oh, he'd managed to say the one thing that made resistance harder. "Clark didn't tell me you'd said yes."

"I told him I wanted to tell you myself. Surprise you at the end of tonight. I've seen you, and Chief, and Melba, and even JJ when you talk about going to church. I want to know what it is you all have over there. I just don't know how to try it or if it will stick. But you came up with the perfect introduction, didn't you? Doesn't that count for something to you?"

Lord, couldn't he be a jerk or something? You know me, I'm going to go all optimistic and hopeful now and

I'm having enough trouble thinking practically already. "If we're going to be…" She didn't know how to finish that sentence without revealing how very attractive she found him, and Jesse surely needed no encouragement in that department.

"Hey," he said, taking her hand. She knew she ought to pull away, but she couldn't muster up the resistance. "Who actually knows what we're going to be? I'm not so sure why you have to plot this out right now. Can't we just wait and see?"

He meant well, but Charlotte knew herself, and she had a bad habit of throwing herself headlong into relationships that ought never to have been pursued. It didn't take a rocket scientist to know there was some serious chemistry between them, and that could make it hard to pull back before it was too late. "Well, the term *playing with fire* does come to mind."

"I'm a fireman. I think we'll be safe. How about I finish my coffee and leave like the gentleman I am? I'll see you at the talent show tomorrow night, and maybe we can try a dinner Sunday. Someplace easy and friendly, like Dellio's."

Those events—she refused to call them dates, even in her head—felt safe.

"I won't even be sitting near you at the talent show. There'll be something like sixty people between us. Then at dinner we can talk some more," he continued. "I can hear you say grace again."

If he was willing to come to church and be part of the talent show, if he was willing to let her say grace over burgers in public, there had to be an openness to faith about him. He was putting in an effort; she ought to at least meet him halfway on this. "Okay."

Jesse finished his coffee in one gulp—something

she'd seen Melba's fireman husband do, so it must be a professional requirement—then stood up to leave. She stood up, as well.

He held his hand out, an oversize request for a formal handshake. "Friendly, see?"

When she offered her hand, he pulled it to his lips and left a soft kiss there. "Well, mostly." Without any further explanation than that, Jesse gathered up his things and headed out the door.

Jesse stood in his kitchen, staring at the still unemptied grocery bags, sorting through the puzzle of his feelings. Exactly what had happened tonight? He knew how to wow a lady, always had. It was an extension— however egotistical—of his urge to please people. He liked making customers happy, helping fire victims, making women feel special.

Whatever it was he felt for Charlotte, it was a whole new thing. He found himself disturbingly desperate for her—but not at all in a physical sense; it was so much more than that. This was much more consuming than a merely physical attraction. There was some gaping, empty hole he couldn't seem to hide from her. Worse, not only could she see it, she effortlessly filled it. As he paced his kitchen, Jesse had the uncomfortable sensation that his life had just cracked open to make room for her and nothing else would ever fill the space that made.

He tried to tell himself that urge to make her happy, to watch the delight spark up in her eyes, was ordinary, an ego boost, the way it was with everyone else. Only with Charlotte, it wasn't. It was the closest thing to a purely selfless urge he'd ever had, and he had no idea what to do with that. Oh, sure, lots of people thought of his work at the firehouse as selfless, but it really wasn't.

It was a hero thing. He liked playing the hero—the stakes at the firehouse were just a bit higher than when he built someone the garage of their dreams.

The old Jesse would have kissed her again even when he knew better. He'd never, ever have pressed his advantage with a woman, but he would have been far bolder than he was tonight. It was as if someone had changed the rules on him without notice.

Without his consent. Chief Bradens really was right: Charlotte hadn't learned how to go in small steps—not in relationships or renovations or maybe even in life. Could he be the man to show her how to slow things down? Lighten up and have a little more fun? Learn that a few dates and kisses could be just that—a few dates and kisses? It was worth a dinner at Dellio's to find out.

And beyond that…he'd figure it out when he got there.

Chapter Twelve

Well, who would have guessed it?

Jesse stood on the stage of Gordon Falls Community Church's meeting hall, hand on the microphone, about to open the church's talent show as its guest emcee and baffled by the open welcome in all the faces he could see. He'd thought of himself as an intruder—an impostor up here on the stage, where someone well-known in the church should have been. No one else seemed to see it that way. Everyone had been nothing but warm and friendly.

"Good evening and welcome to tonight's Taste of Talent. If you haven't filled your plate from the dessert table at the back of the room, you don't know what you're missing. And hey, if any of you find yourselves overcome with the urge to bring me some of that raspberry cheesecake, by all means don't hold back." He couldn't help himself from directing that last remark right at Charlotte.

Instead of feeling awkward, the past half hour of setup had been surprisingly fun. What he'd told Charlotte was true; he'd never had anything against going to the church. So many of his friends already did. It was just that he dreaded the hurdle of that first visit. By happenstance—or design—this gig handed him the perfect opening. "We're going to start things out tonight with a touch of class, and a lot of brass. Let's listen to the Senior High bell quartet."

He looked out over the sea of friendly faces from his stool at stage left, seeing proud, smiling parents among them. Honestly, even here he felt like a bit of a celebrity—and he was a man given to enjoying attention. "Aren't they talented?" he asked the audience, as the quartet cleared their many bells from the stage. "There's more where that came from. This is one talented congregation, I'm telling you. Here's what's up next…"

And so the evening progressed, act by surprising act. Jesse's initial comments about the flood of talent were just to be nice at first, playing to the audience. Eventually, they gave way to genuine astonishment, soundly trouncing Jesse's preconceptions of hokey church festivities. Max Jones, Charlotte's cousin and no stranger to the firehouse through his sister, JJ, did a hysterical lip-synch of an Elvis tune with the high school boy he'd been mentoring for almost a year, Simon Williams. "Talk about true rocking and rolling," Jesse cracked as the pair—who both used wheelchairs—popped a dual pair of wheelies and spins as they moved offstage. Jesse felt a warm glow as he watched Simon's dad, Brian, also a firefighter, give his son a standing ovation. The kid had come a long way, and he knew that Brian credited the support of this church as much as the partnership Simon had with Max. Jesse and Max—and a few of the other younger firefighters—had made a few mistakes in their efforts to help Simon, but everyone had learned their lesson, and even Simon's mom had given Jesse a warm welcome.

And where had Fire Marshal Chad Owens hidden his surprising juggling talents? He was normally a laid-back guy, but the audience hung their mouths open when he proved a pretty talented trickster. Those open mouths served them well, for Chad's finale was to juggle a dozen of his wife, Jeannie's, beloved chocolate caramels, tossing them into the audience as his final trick. Jesse would have eaten a handful if the sticky confections wouldn't have rendered him speechless for five minutes at least. He stuck with one, making a big show of chewing with the appropriate *mmm*s. "Well now," he managed, still sounding as if he had a mouthful, "guess they really meant it when they called this Taste of Talent."

There were other acts—some silly, some heartwarming. Even the regrettable ones—someone needed to tell Nick Owens an eleven-minute drum solo was hard on the ears—brought a smile and a hearty round of applause from the audience. The trio of curly-blond-haired girls who couldn't have been more than five didn't do much more than sway and spin in their frilly pink tutus, but no one cared. Instead, everyone cheered and snapped photos like paparazzi when the ballerinas took their bows, bursting into louder applause, mixed with laughter, when one little girl rushed over and hugged Jesse's leg, leading him to take her hand and twirl her like a ballroom dancer as she left the stage.

Every time Jesse thought the evening couldn't get more enjoyable, some new moment would capture his heart. He was having such a terrific time, Jesse decided he'd have to eat his words and thank Charlotte for pulling him in to the event. Charlotte must have been thinking the same thing, for every time he caught her eyes, her smile broadcast "See, I told you this would be fun."

What really brought the house down, however, was one of the final acts. Jesse knew JJ's husband, Alex, played the ukulele and was known for his campy musical sense. As such, it wasn't a big stunner when he took the stage and began strumming "By the Light of the Silvery Moon." What no one saw coming was when Violet Sharpton and Karl Kennedy—of Karl's Koffee fame—sashayed onstage and broke into a snappy duet. No one knew either of them could sing, but they were fabulous. When they added an adorable half-limped, cane-assisted little soft-shoe dance on the final verse, Karl yelping, "Slow down, son, I can't hoof it that fast with my bad hip," to a guffawing Alex, the crowd spared no effort to urge them on. They got a standing ovation, and deserved one. Jesse himself was smiling and laughing so hard he could barely take the microphone as the curtain behind him closed.

"I don't know how we're going to follow that act, folks," Jesse proclaimed, wiping his eyes. He hid his satisfaction at the frantic scrambling behind him from the other side of the curtain. "Oh, no, wait," he said in mock surprise. "As a matter of fact, I do." Drums behind him hit the *ba-dump-ching* that was the standard musical punctuation for bad jokes, and Jesse knew his own surprise was nearly ready. He'd successfully managed to keep his contribution a secret. If a church was going to ask him to emcee a talent show, they'd better be prepared for what they got.

A hidden set of drums began a steady beat behind him. "Ladies and gentlemen, presenting for the first time ever on this or any stage, for your listening enjoyment…"

A base guitar joined in with a bluesy swagger. "I give you…Jesse Sykes and the Red Suspenders!"

The curtain parted to reveal a band composed entirely of hidden talents from the Gordon Falls Volunteer Fire Department, decked out in black shirts and those cheesy red plastic fire helmets Wally's sister had found at the local party store. And, of course, red suspenders. The applause and laughter from the audience was enough to fuel Jesse's gloat for a month.

It had started out as a joke, a wisecrack from Yorky when they found out Jesse had been cornered into serving as the evening's master of ceremonies. A "wouldn't it be funny if…" that took on more and more momentum until the idea seemed too good to pass up. When Wally shared that he played the drums and Tom Matthews offered to fish his bass guitar out of the attic, the Red Suspenders were born. Jesse reached behind him, knowing Tom held out his next props. As the lead guitar riff began, the hoots of encouragement and surprise doubled. When Jesse donned the red hat and a pair of sunglasses, the crowd went wild. Chief Bradens was laughing so hard he was alternating between wiping his eyes and hiding them.

Going to great lengths to rehearse in secret, the guys had worked out a squeaky-clean, church-worthy four-song list that dipped into gospel, soul and just enough rock to enthrall the youth group. By the second song, the audience was clapping along. By the third song, they were on their feet. When the bass guitar and drums kicked into the familiar introduction to "Stand by Me," Jesse was pretty sure he saw Charlotte go pink. This was going to be fun.

Charlotte watched Jesse up there on that stage and felt her heart run off against her wishes. She didn't want to be falling for this boisterous, all-too-charming fire-man, but there didn't seem to be much she could do to stop it. Melba sat next to her and would catch her eye after this remark or that heart-slaying grin, and she tried to feel neutral about the guy. Clearly Melba could see she was failing. Of course, Melba had no qualms about pairing off with a man from the fire department, even if she was kind about Charlotte's resistance.

Charlotte had gone so far as to talk to Clark about it. Clark had grown up in a firefighting family—the son of the former chief—and he had freely shared that things had been hard on his mom. He told her he understood her hesitation and respected it. "I remember how much my mom had to endure," he said. "I understand why you'd choose to avoid it. I'll say this, though. If the right guy comes around and happens to wear a uniform, I think you'll find a way to handle it."

Charlotte was terrified the right guy was standing right in front of her. She shut her eyes for a moment, even as she felt Jesse's presence from the distance across the room. Jesse was dead wrong about a crowded room making being with him any safer. *Lord, You know the effect that man has on me. If this isn't where I should be heading, I'm going to need an escape. I'm losing perspective.*

Melba leaned over and whispered in Charlotte's ear, "He keeps looking right at you, doesn't he? I mean, it sure looks like it."

That was not helpful. Charlotte had spent the past twenty minutes trying to tell herself the sensation of Jesse singling her out in the crowd was just an emotional illusion. The trick of a good entertainer—an *amazing* entertainer, really, Charlotte admitted to herself as she watched him sing on the stage, backed up by the rest of the Red Suspenders. The combination of silly plastic fire hat and bad-boy black sunglasses was downright irresistible.

As the band began the introduction from what Charlotte knew had to be "Stand by Me," Jesse took off his sunglasses and made a show of peering into the crowd. Charlotte told herself to slump down in her chair, useless as that tactic might be. Her breath—which had momentarily stopped—let out when Jesse called, "Maria? Maria Bradens? Where are you, darlin'? I know you like this one."

Oh, please let him just play this to Maria. Don't let him realize what his voice singing this does to me.

"Home with the sitter!" Clark called back, laughing.

That was right. Maria wasn't even in the building. With a pulse that ricocheted between fear and thrill, Charlotte watched as Jesse unhitched the cordless microphone from its stand. He stared straight at Charlotte, those high-voltage eyes at full force. "Well now, I'll need someone else. Another fine young lady who might be partial to this song." His voice was silken, all confidence and charisma as he stepped down off the stage and began walking right toward her. "Any takers?"

Charlotte felt as if her cheeks were as red as his hat. She tried to hide her face behind her hands but Melba pulled them down. As the fireman behind the keyboard launched into the song, Jesse passed his hat to Clark, pulled Charlotte to her feet and began to sing the lyrics, about not being afraid even when the night was dark. It was as if he sang directly to every fear and every worry. His voice seemed to find every bit of resistance she was trying to hang on to, every memory of her mother alone and staring at the unused place setting on their kitchen table. He was pulling all the stops out, pulling her under in the process.

When he turned back toward the stage, Charlotte practically fell into the chair. She'd forgotten how to think. She'd forgotten how to breathe. When he pitched his voice up into a soulful wail for the second verse, showing a level of talent she'd never expected—nor had anyone else, from the level of applause that was roaring up from the audience—she'd have followed him anywhere.

And that, right there, was the problem. *He is irresistible.*

What he did next hit Charlotte as clearly as if someone had tossed a glass of water in her face. Two rows down, Jesse found the high school French teacher and began singing to her. The woman looked exactly as Charlotte had felt when she'd been in that position: dazzled. Jesse asked her how to say "Stand by Me" in French and began singing the chorus in French, even getting her to sing with him.

Was his attention—the attention that, a moment ago she thought was just for her—an act? She watched the woman lay her hand on her chest and sigh, realizing she'd done the exact same thing herself. When he picked a third woman out of the audience and charmed her just as effectively, a foolish, hollow feeling crept up Charlotte's chest. She had no idea if Jesse was genuine in his attention to her, genuine in his attention to each woman he'd singled out of the audience, or simply applying his talents at showmanship.

Either way, it drove home a point she'd managed to miss—or chose to miss. Hadn't Jesse made it clear after that kiss back at the cottage that he felt no pressure for them to be serious? She'd been too dazed then to recognize what he was really saying—just as she was barely clearheaded enough now to realize the truth.

He wasn't ready to *offer* her anything serious.

Jesse, who displayed so much of his charm but hid so much of his nature, who gave away his talents but locked up his dreams, who was as impressed by her drive as he was bewildered by it, didn't know how to truly, deeply commit. Not to God, not to a woman, not to his business plans that never seemed to get off the ground—not even to just one woman when it came to dedicating a special song.

Worse yet, part of her didn't even care. Even in the face of all her reservations, he enthralled her as he caught her eyes one last time before he stepped back up onto the stage. Despite everything she just saw, her breath caught as it felt as though he was singing just to her.

Charlotte was defenseless. The past few minutes had startled her into the awareness that she would fall for him far too easily—and get her heart broken when he stopped short of returning that love. On her good days, her resistance might stand up for a while. On a bad day, she'd give in instantly. Hadn't his kiss in her kitchen proved that? Her attraction to Jesse overrode her good sense even when she tried to stop it. With a gulp she realized that if he had tried to kiss her right in the middle of that song, with his eyes pulling her in like that, she very well might have let him, and returned it with the same intensity if not more. In front of everyone. Despite all the reasons she knew she didn't want to get involved with him. Because she *wanted* to get involved with him. She hadn't stopped thinking about him. She'd always imagined herself falling that hard for the perfect guy—and Jesse Sykes was not the perfect guy. He was a great guy, an amazing guy, but he was not the right guy for her.

Sure, it was impulsive. It was probably even cowardly and childish, but none of that stopped Charlotte from making the quickest exit possible while the crowd moved toward the stage to congratulate the Red Suspenders for stealing the show.

She was glad she'd walked to the church tonight, grateful for the space and dark and calm to help sort out her thoughts. Jesse was magnetic—in every sense the word implied. As she worked the brand-new lock on her front door, she recalled the unsettling realization she'd come to the other night: her extravagant renovation plans were partially to keep Jesse around.

Lord, I'm a mess. I'm getting all tangled up here. Help!

As she dropped her handbag in the hallway, her cell phone rang. She didn't even have to look at the screen to know it was Jesse. "Hey, where'd you go?" He sounded so exuberant.

"I'm home."

"Home? You went home?"

"I'm sorry," she replied, leaning against the wall without even switching on the light. "Look, that was just a bit much for me."

She heard him push out a breath. "What? The song? I know you like that one. I was just having fun."

Could he have picked worse words? "Just having fun."

"Wait, what's wrong here? Did I embarrass you? I'm

sorry if I did that, okay? I thought you'd like it. I like singing to you. You looked like you were having fun."

She couldn't help her reply. "Oh, they were all having fun, I'm sure. You're quite the showman."

Someone tried to grab his attention, and she heard Jesse shoo them away. "Are you upset that I sang to you in front of everyone like that?"

She wasn't, and that was part of the problem. "No. It's just… I don't know. I just wanted to get out of there, okay?"

"No, it's not okay. I'm not quite sure what I did wrong here, but I don't want to leave it like this. Talk to me. Better yet, give me ten minutes and I'll be over there."

"No, don't." She squeezed her eyes shut, knowing what a stab that might be but then wondering—with the way he was always careful to hide what he was feeling— if that would be any kind of a dent to him at all.

"I'm at a loss here, Charlotte. C'mon, talk to me."

"It's… I'm okay. Stunned, maybe. Give me time."

"I sang to lots of people. But I especially sang to you. We've got a history with that song, don't we? Wait… are you upset that I didn't sing it only to you? Is that what this is about?"

It sounded so petty, so hopelessly infatuated when he said it, that Charlotte cringed and sank against the wall. There was more to it than that, but she couldn't put it into words. She couldn't even answer him.

"Whoa. It's not like that. It was an impulse, an entertainer thing." After a moment he said, "I'm a jerk. A show-off. Let's talk about this. Dinner tomorrow, right?"

It wouldn't help. She'd just see his eyes and the whole tumbling would start all over again.

"Charlotte…don't make this into something it wasn't. If you won't let me come over there now, at least let's do dinner like we planned."

"I just need to…I don't know, sort this out somehow. Good night, Jesse, you were amazing. Really, really amazing."

She heard him fending off someone else, then come back to the phone. "Dinner. I'm not hanging up until you agree to dinner."

She didn't have the nerve to fight him off right now. "Okay. Dinner." She ended the call.

Would anything change in twenty-four hours? Was she being fair if she didn't allow Jesse a chance to explain himself? Charlotte had no idea. Half an hour of sitting still and trying to listen for God brought no clarity. Fifteen minutes of petting Mo and staring into his wise yellow eyes didn't help, either. Knitting—her usual solace of preference—lasted less than ten minutes. Finally, in desperation, Charlotte turned on her laptop to look over her e-mail.

There, at the top of her inbox, was an e-mail from Borroughs Yarn and Fabric Supply in Stowe, Vermont. Every knitter knew Borroughs was a great company, a maker of high-quality yarns. Now they were developing an admirable reputation for inventive patterns and clever supplies for all kinds of textile arts. They'd already taken many of the steps she'd been trying to get Monarch to consider in utilizing digital media. Their blog was gaining serious traction—they were getting it right and seeing results. And they were asking her to come out for an interview after the upcoming Fourth of July holiday to discuss the possibility of heading up their new online commerce department.

I need this. Even if I don't get the job, it will put a bit of space between Jesse and I so I can think. Thank You, Lord. I knew You'd make a way.

Charlotte replied that she'd let them know as soon as her flights were booked. Now she'd have something to put some space between her and that charismatic, problematic fireman.

Chapter Thirteen

"Vermont?" Melba looked as shocked as Charlotte had expected her to be.

"Well, just part of the time. Or all of the time if I want it, and the company and I can come to an agreement." They were having a spontaneous post-church picnic on a blanket in Melba's backyard, watching Maria kick and wiggle.

"Vermont?" Melba said again. "And you're actually considering it?"

"I was laid off a month ago today. I've been putting out feelers every day since then, and all I've got to show for it is a few phone interviews that made me feel inept and a stack of carefully worded deflections." Maybe it wasn't such a smart idea to have kept how badly the job search was going from Melba all this time. "There aren't as many jobs out there as I thought there were. Monarch's not the only company feeling the pinch."

"But you're here. You want to be here." Melba scooped up Maria as if to shield her from the news. "Don't you?"

Charlotte sighed. "Of course I do. But I need a job, and there don't seem to be any jobs for me here." It was the first time she'd spoken that truth out loud, and it let loose the growing tendril of fear in the pit of her stomach she'd been trying so hard to ignore. She'd been so sure of her path up until now. So convinced God had led her straight to Gordon Falls.

So sure she never wanted to be attached to someone like Jesse Sykes.

Melba settled Maria into her lap and furrowed her brows. "Did your mom finally get to you?"

Charlotte's mom, usually supportive, had lately begun to express concerns about Charlotte buying the cottage and sinking so much of her inheritance into the renovations. She hadn't said anything during the sale and the first days, but telling comments had started sneaking their way into conversations. A doubt here, a question there, a disapproving silence after renovation updates on the phone. The unspoken current of "and you still don't have a new job" ran constantly under every conversation. "Let's just say she hasn't been enthusiastic in her support."

Normally she didn't let her mother get to her that way, but the undeniable truth was that Charlotte was starting to worry about it herself. The gorgeous high-end kitchen faucet that cost twice as much as the standard—was that really what she needed? The armoire from the antiques store—was that really "the most darling thing she'd ever seen" or had it seemed that way because she'd gotten two rejections that day? The credit card bill had come last night, and it hadn't been pretty. Sure, she had the funds for now, but she couldn't—shouldn't—keep up the spending like this. Things were starting to come unraveled around the edges; she knew it on some level, just didn't know what to do about it.

"Don't let her get to you, Charlotte. You love that house. You belong in that house."

That was still true. Charlotte leaned back on her elbows, admiring the emerald-green of the leaves as they fluttered in the breeze overhead. It was so wonderfully green here. Everything seemed to be thriving—well, everything except her. "I didn't say I was going to sell the house. I just may not get to live here for a while."

"What are you going to do?"

"I'll still finish the renovations, but I might have to rent it out for a while."

Melba twirled a leaf over Maria's head, watching how her eyes followed the shapes and colors. "I can't imagine anyone in that house but you. You can't rent it to just anyone."

"Actually," Charlotte said carefully, keeping her voice as neutral as possible, "I was thinking of asking Jesse if he wanted to rent it. I know he just lives in an apartment now and it might make it easier to finish the renovations."

"Yes." Melba raised her eyebrows. "Let's talk about Jesse. About what's going on between you two. You could have lit half the valley on the sparks flying between you two at the talent show last night."

"He's a showman."

"Yes, he is. But while he sang to some other people, it was a whole different thing when he sang to you. And you still haven't told me about Friday's dinner in your kitchen. I want to hear it all—everything from dinner to why you disappeared after the talent show."

Bit by bit, Charlotte unfolded the entire story of dinner at the cottage. It felt useful to put the thing into words, to try and describe—if she couldn't hope to explain—what had sprung up between her and Jesse.

Melba's response was an unlikely mix of surprise and "I told you so." She, of all people, could understand the pile of conflict mounting in Charlotte's heart.

"Wow," she said when Charlotte finished her tale and fell flat on her back on the blanket. "I mean, really, wow. This is a side of Jesse I don't think anyone's ever seen. He's mostly just a goofball around the firehouse, but it seems the man is an insufferable romantic."

Charlotte put her hands over her eyes, the vision of Jesse's magnetic gaze heating her cheeks all over again. "So what if he is? That doesn't mean he's capable of—or even looking for—commitment. Come on, your own husband called him 'an insufferable bachelor.' I don't want to be just another member of the Jesse Sykes fan club."

"I'm sure you can tell the difference."

"No, I can't. Not yet," Charlotte admitted, rolling onto her stomach to bury her face in the blanket. "I was defenseless when he sang to me in my kitchen, too. 'You Send Me' while he made the Alfredo sauce."

"The Sam Cooke song? I think I'd melt right into the Alfredo."

"I'm pretty sure I did. And the kiss…" She rolled back over and draped her hand over her face dramatically. "Glory, but that man can kiss. I was a goner. If it hadn't been for Mo, I'd have been in serious trouble. I *am* in serious trouble." She sat up. "That's what makes it so hard—I can't tell what's genuine. If he was just a guy on the make, I don't think he would have backed off when I asked him to in my kitchen. There's really something there. But you saw what he did to those other women in the audience. I don't know what's real. I'm not even sure he knows."

"I don't, either, but I'm pretty sure moving to Vermont isn't the answer."

"But it could be. I've lost my job and Mima. I'm not in a good place to think smart right now."

"Have you talked to him about any of this?"

"We were going to talk at dinner tonight, but he called me earlier and said he got pulled onto duty and we have to postpone. What if some time and distance is exactly what I need? The cottage will still be here in a year, and I'll be stronger."

"And Jesse? What if he's not here?"

That would be okay, wouldn't it? That would mean God had helped her shut a door she wasn't strong enough to shut on her own. That was what she'd prayed for, what she'd come to understand as the opportunity this Vermont job offer presented. Only if that were true, where was that sense of assurance, that ability to leap forward that had always been her strength? "Then I'll know it wasn't supposed to work out."

Melba gave her a doubtful stare. "You need to talk to him, Charlotte. You need to tell him in person that you're thinking about the Vermont offer. You need to ask him outright what's going on between the two of you."

"I know. I know. We'll have dinner tomorrow and I'll do it then."

Chapter Fourteen

There was a reason most firefighters hated the Fourth of July.

It was as if the world was ganging up on him to make sure he didn't have enough time to think through what was going on with Charlotte. Three false alarms, two parades, multiple firecracker-related incidents and four guys sick on the squad. As Jesse was fond of joking, "Some weeks it just didn't pay to be a volunteer firefighter." And that wasn't even counting the two construction jobs that were stymied by the holiday and back-ordered supplies.

He'd used the time away from Charlotte to go over that night at the talent show a dozen times in his head. It wasn't as if he'd planned what he was going to do when he went into the audience, but the way Charlotte looked at him had practically pulled him offstage. He loved what his voice did to her eyes, the way his touch could raise color in her cheeks. They had such a strong connection that he felt just a bit out of control when he sang to her.

That wasn't how it was supposed to happen. The leap in his gut made him pull back, made him resort to old tricks and play up to other women in the audience. He'd known exactly what he was doing when he'd shifted his attention to the high school teacher, had even guessed how Charlotte would react. It didn't surprise him that the other women were as entertained as Charlotte was. It did stun him that he didn't enjoy their blushing smiles. He'd walked back to the stage that night not wanting to sing the final chorus to anyone but Charlotte. That was not who Jesse Sykes was. He wasn't ready to be so serious with Charlotte, or with any one woman right now.

Still, he couldn't stay away. The tone of her voice—the hurt and confusion when they'd spoken on the phone—echoed in his head no matter how hard he tried to shake it off. He told himself it was okay, maybe even a good thing, that things felt off-kilter when they'd talked. It was for the best that things had cooled off considerably when he was forced to postpone their date for Dellio's until after the Fourth. This unpredictability was part of his life, part of why he couldn't get serious with a woman. It was better that they'd have to take separate cars, because he was still wearing a beeper tonight, on call in case one of the other firefighters called in sick with whatever nasty bug was still making its way around the firehouse.

If he got called in out of their dinner, the interruption would be a sore spot for Charlotte. Still, the firehouse and its demands were part of who he was. If anything were ever to work out between them, they'd have to figure this part out. He just didn't know if that was possible. He still wanted to take this in small steps, and he just didn't know if Charlotte was capable of small steps in anything.

Even though it had been his idea, Jesse found Dellio's an annoying opposite of their first dinner. It was a local favorite; a noisy, greasy, delicious diner—one of the few places Jesse felt produced burgers nearly as good as his own. And the French fries? They were legendary—everybody loved them.

She was waiting in his favorite booth. That had to be a good sign. Despite all the complications, he still wanted tonight to go well, still wanted to move things forward and halt the backward slide they'd taken. Other women had never wandered continually into his thoughts like this—even on the job, where he used to be known for his single-minded focus.

"Glad you finally made it." She was trying to make a joke of it, to keep things light, but it was clear the long postponement had hit a nerve.

"Yeah." He surprised himself by hiding the beeper in his pocket and switching it to Vibrate so that she wouldn't see he was on call. *Cut her some slack, okay, God?* He was equally surprised to feel the tiny prayer rise up out of him, hoping the God she spoke to so easily had enough kindness not to rub salt in the wound tonight. *No calls—I'd consider it a favor.* He switched subjects. "How's Mo settling in?"

"Generous of you to ask, considering. He's doing okay. He hasn't broken or shredded anything, if that's what you mean, but there isn't a lot to shred just yet. I can't really hang curtains downstairs until the new windows get installed."

Of course she had to mention the back-ordered windows. "They'll be here in ten days, they tell me. The two new doors are supposed to come in tomorrow, along with the closet fixtures, so I can get started on those as soon as things calm down." She'd ordered top-of-the-line interior doors for the upstairs bedrooms, but the master bedroom closet was the thing that really stunned him. She'd moved one wall and taken a corner of the upstairs hallway to build out what she termed "a decent-sized closet." Jesse would have considered something half that size "decent." This was edging closer to decadent. And expensive. She'd gotten defensive when he made even the tiniest remark about the cost.

"The sink's working great, and everything in the bathroom is just perfect." She was picking at the edge of her menu with one fingernail.

"Glad to hear it. That tub looks just as good as a new one, don't you think?" *Come on, you're supposed to be patching things up with the lady and the only conversation you can manage is plumbing fixtures?*

"It was a good idea. I've got a few more ideas I want to try out on you, but let's order first."

Things eased up once the food came, but while he waited for her to bring up the subject of the talent-show night, she failed to raise the topic. Should he bring it up first? That didn't feel right—it was mostly her issue; he should follow her lead.

Instead, Charlotte said a quiet grace over the food—not as long as the prayer she'd said over their previous dinner, but it had the same effect on him. To be continually thankful like that—over something as mundane as burgers and fries—it got to him. When she added a plea for safety for Jesse and all the Gordon Falls Volunteer Fire Department, his heart did a startling twist in his chest as if the prayer had physically embedded itself there. Her voice took on a different quality, soft and lush, lively and yet peaceful at the same time. Jesse found himself easily and even gladly saying "Amen" to her blessing over the food.

The effortlessness he was so drawn to in her cottage came back to their conversation bit by bit. Maybe things had settled on their own—and that was okay, wasn't it? He didn't want to make this more complicated than it already was. That smile—the one that managed to tumble his insides in a matter of seconds—came back. Still, it was easy to see she had a lot on her mind, and at some point they were going to talk about whatever went haywire between them the other night.

"So." He decided to press the issue when they were halfway through the heart-attack-on-a-plate hamburgers and they still hadn't talked about whatever she needed to say. "What's up?"

"You mentioned your apartment lease was nearly up the other day." He'd expected a deluge of emotional questions and concerns, not that. She fiddled nervously with a French fry, drawing artistic circles in the puddle of ketchup on her plate. What was going on?

"I did," he replied slowly, cautiously.

"I don't know if you'd find this at all appealing, but if I ended up taking a job offer out of town, would you consider renting the cottage for a year?"

Where had that come from? And what did a question like that mean given everything that had gone on between them? "You're leaving?"

"No. I mean, I don't know. What if I have to? It hasn't…well, it hasn't been as easy to find a new job as I'd hoped."

If this was about how he'd behaved at the talent show, the cottage was no place to take it out on him. Rent? Why? "Well, sure it's a tough market out there, but…" It surprised him how much the thought of her leaving stung him.

"I don't want to spend my days marketing widgets just because it's the only marketing job I can do from home. I want to work in the fiber industry. Textiles at the very least. There are only so many companies big enough to hire. I've gone a whole month with no serious prospects. Now there is one in Vermont that's starting to sound promising and...well...I may need to go where the work is."

This seemed a hundred miles from the impulsive, passionate Charlotte of just a few days ago. He reminded himself that she'd wanted to slow things down. She'd put the brakes on their relationship, and he was happy about that. Wasn't he? That didn't explain the irrational annoyance climbing up his spine. He hadn't wanted to get serious with anyone, least of all her, so he knew he shouldn't be ticked that she was considering an out-of-town offer. It made no sense. "I suppose that makes sense," he said, just because he couldn't come up with anything else to say.

"What do you think?"

Was she asking him if he'd take the lease? Or was she looking for him to ask her to stay? How was he supposed to know the right answer to a question like that—especially after the other night? He sat back in the booth. "Are you leaving?" The words made her flinch just a bit—they'd come out sharper than he would have liked.

"I just said I don't know yet. I don't want to go—" she gave the words an emphasis that made Jesse's insides tumble in eight different directions "—but what if I don't have a choice?"

"You always have a choice, Charlotte. If you really want to stay here, then you can find a way to make it happen." He looked at her. "Vermont? You don't really strike me as the rural New England type." He knew it wouldn't sit well, but he had to ask anyway. "So now you're sorry you bought the cottage?" If she were to walk away from it now, it would feel like rubbing salt on the wound she'd dealt him by buying it out from under him in the first place.

"No. I'm not sorry. I'm not saying Vermont's perfect, but it may have to do for a little while. And I don't want to sell the cottage. I'll want to come back to it. I love it and I want to keep going on the work on it. But I can't stomach the idea of just anyone living there."

So I'm a convenient stand-in? "I'm not so sure that would work." It was time she knew the full story. It was clear she needed to know. "Look, Charlotte, you should know that this hasn't exactly been a cakewalk for me seeing you in that house. I'd been plotting to buy the cottage for months before you showed up."

Surprise widened her eyes. Maybe now she'd understand why this might be an especially touchy subject.

"The reason why I have all those good ideas on what needs to be done is that I've been thinking about it all year. I just needed two more months to save up enough for the down payment. Not all of us get windfalls from loving grandmothers, you know."

Windfalls from loving grandmothers? The edge in Jesse's words cut off Charlotte's breath. Did he realize how hurtful that sounded?

"The home you were going to buy to launch your business was my cottage?" Suddenly everything that had transpired between them became suspicious, as if he'd been working some hidden agenda she wasn't clever enough to notice. Was it so hard to believe he'd played to her just as he played to other women in the audience—that she was just a customer like any other—after hearing that fact?

"Was. So you can see that renting it from you might be a bit of a touchy business for me?"

"Why didn't you say anything about this before?" It made no sense that he'd keep it from her unless there was some reason behind his silence.

He pinched the bridge of his nose. "Leave me just a little bit of pride in this, won't you? I didn't have any legal claim to the cottage—I just hadn't moved fast enough when you struck like lightning. The gracious loser thing doesn't come easily to me. I figured it'd just make things uncomfortable between us if I brought it up."

"So if you couldn't be the owner, you'd get the owner as your biggest customer, is that it?" She began to think through every decision he'd encouraged or discouraged, wondering if his charming helpfulness was ever fully genuine.

"No, that's not it." He planted his hands on the table, his eyes darkening at the accusation. "My offer to help was mostly on the level."

Well, that was a telling choice of words. "Mostly?"

"Of course I saw it as a good business opportunity. Your house represented a big job for me, and I needed a big job. I won't say I wasn't ticked at first. I was. But you clearly needed help, and I knew that I was the best guy for the job. And it wasn't long before it became more than business. You know that." He tossed his napkin on the table, and for a moment she wondered if he'd simply stand up and walk out. He didn't.

Instead, he leaned in. "I'd procrastinated on my plans too long and it came back to bite me—that's not a new lesson for me. This one just hurt a bit more than the others, and maybe that's good." His eyes took on that intense quality that always pulled her in, always made her heart skip. "Charlotte, you belong in that house. Every time I said that I meant it. You belong there. Why on earth are you leaving it? Leaving here?"

At that moment, it struck her that she was waiting to hear "Why are you leaving *me?*" Only that was not what he said, and that omission said everything. "I don't know that I'm leaving. I don't want to leave. But if I can't find a job here, I may not have a choice. I'm just trying to find a good solution for the property if I have to go." She paused, struck again by the enormity of his omission. How could he spend so much time with her in that place and keep his original intentions from her? It felt so manipulative. All the intensity of his persuasion at dinner, his attentions at the talent show, they all felt fabricated now.

"So that's what I am? A useful solution?"

She was not using him. She'd made the suggestion to be helpful. Yes, to both of them, but she hadn't used him the way he'd used her. "That's not fair. I didn't know you wanted the cottage. And the reason I didn't know was because you hid it from me."

"What, exactly, would have been the point of telling you? The only thing it would have done was made things awkward. As it was, things were pretty great." He ran one hand down his face. "Well, to tell the truth, I don't know what things are right now." His phone vibrated loudly in his pocket. "I thought we had something going on at dinner the other night, and I thought we had fun at the talent show, but how it got all serious and complicated all of a sudden is beyond me." His phone continued to go off and he grumbled while he fished it out.

This whole thing was a mess. "Jesse…"

Jesse practically threw the device on the table as

the firehouse sirens began to wail through the night air. Charlotte realized it wasn't his phone at all, but the firehouse beeper. "You're on duty?"

"I'm on call," he growled. "And now I have to go in." He muttered a few unkind words under his breath as he slid out of the booth and tossed a pair of twenty-dollar bills on the table. "We're going to have to finish this—whatever this is—another time."

Charlotte stared at her food, the delectable burger having lost all its appeal. Jesse couldn't have picked a worse moment to be called into the firehouse. She tried to summon a prayer of sympathy for whoever's home or business was facing the threat of fire, but self-pity overpowered her better nature. Right now, she selfishly despised the siren.

Here, in a single moment, was every reason why she and Jesse wouldn't work. They didn't consider the same things important. He should have told her the minute they'd sat down that he was on call. He should have told her he'd been eyeing the cottage before she bought it.

He should have told her he wanted her to stay in Gordon Falls.

I got it all wrong, Mima. This isn't what you would have wanted. You were looking to give me adventure and I turned it into foolishness. If I had only waited, thought some more about what I was doing, I wouldn't be in this mess.

She fought the urge to do something, to move or talk or do anything to stem the discomfort now crawling under her skin as if her emotional state had taken on physical symptoms. *Sit and think, don't react,* she told herself, but it didn't help. She was a whole ball of reaction.

Charlotte ate two more bites of her burger before giving up. She flagged the server and asked to have both meals boxed up, grateful most of the Dellio's staff was familiar with the firehouse and used to people dashing out midmeal. She added a few more bills to cover the tip and left the restaurant, knowing she'd hold the sight of that half-empty booth with two meals in her head for a long, long time. One person with two plates of food—how she knew and detested that view.

She made sure her route home didn't take her past the firehouse. When she pulled into her driveway, the glow through the curtainless front windows looked forlorn instead of expectant. The house that had always spoken of possibilities struck her tonight as a giant pile of things undone. The feeling she'd fought off since she'd signed the sale papers rose up huge and undeniable. It was clear now that she'd bitten off far more than she could chew.

I need to think this through.

She knew, as strongly as she recognized the truth, that she needed time and space away from Jesse and Gordon Falls in order to do that.

Charlotte stood in the hallway, half paralyzed with indecision, half desperate to do something. She tried to pray but she had no idea what to pray for. *I need something to do, Lord. I can't just stand here.*

With no visible path, Charlotte simply kept doing the next thing that came to mind. First, she turned the oven on low and tucked the food in to keep it warm until her hunger returned. Then she put the kettle on to make a cup of tea. While she drank the tea, she opened up her laptop and booked the flight to Vermont. Then, in what felt like the first clear thought of the night, she packed her bag to head back to the Chicago apartment. It'd be easier to catch a cab to the airport from there, and she needed to be gone when Jesse got off duty.

She picked up the cat carrier Melba had brought for Mo and opened the door. "If we leave now, we'll be in Chicago a little before ten. We'll figure out tomorrow when tomorrow comes." Astonishingly, the cat walked right in as if he thought that was a smart idea. What more encouragement did she need? She was packed and turning onto the highway before an hour had passed.

Chapter Fifteen

Jesse winced as the emergency room doctor wrapped the plastic splint around his swollen ankle. "Is it a bad break?" He'd seen the X-ray and could guess, but he wanted confirmation.

"I've seen worse. If you stay off it—and I mean really off it, no weight on that ankle for three days until the swelling goes down enough to put a hard cast on it—you'll be back in action in six weeks."

"Six weeks?" Jesse moaned and let his head fall back against the examining bed, listening to its paper cover crinkle in sanitary sympathy.

The doctor peered over the top of his glasses. "You could be off crutches and into a walking cast in three or four weeks if it heals well. But if you push it and try to go faster, you could end up needing surgery. You may need surgery anyway." He peered again at the bandage on Jesse's leg. It covered a nasty gash just above the break. "Come back tomorrow to get the dressing changed. We'll see how the swelling has gone down by then. Ice every twenty minutes, ibuprofen for the pain, keep it elevated, you know the drill."

Chief Bradens pulled aside the curtain, looking

weary. "Another down. What the flu started, that porch railing finished. I'm going to have to call another department to send a few guys to hold us over until some of the others are back on their feet."

"Sorry." Jesse knew injuries were part of the job, and no one could have foreseen that the porch railing wouldn't hold when he tripped and fell into it. Some small part of him—the part that keenly remembered Charlotte's prayer for his safety not hours before—knew he was fortunate not to have been more badly hurt. Still, a larger and angrier part of him was ticked off at all the trouble this break would cause.

"Come on, Sykes, it's not your fault. I'm just glad you'll be okay to come back eventually."

"Sure, in mid-August."

"More like September, actually," the doctor cut in. "You'll need another two weeks of physical therapy after getting the cast off to get back into enough shape to go out on call."

"And let's not even talk about my time off the job," Jesse moaned. Mondale wouldn't take kindly to having to call someone else in to finish his jobs. Someone else working on Charlotte's cottage? And the loss of income? Even with insurance, it would set his plan for the launch of Sykes Homes back a month if not more. Tonight was turning out to be a lousy evening on every front.

"Let's worry about that tomorrow and get you home." Chief Bradens began the paperwork while Jesse hoisted himself up with the pair of crutches that would be his constant companions for the next few weeks. "Have you got someone who can help you out tonight?"

His mom would be here in minutes if he called. Even Randy, busy as he was, might find a way to stay overnight if asked. Only Jesse didn't want any of those people. He wanted Charlotte. Despite everything that was getting tangled further between them, the urge to do his recuperating in that overstuffed old plaid chair in the corner of Charlotte's living room came over him like a craving. He'd even put up with Mo to spend his days sitting on that chair watching her putter around the house with that elated, decor-planning look on her face. Go figure.

That option, however, was off the table for now if not forever.

"I'm set," he hedged, knowing the chief himself would find someone to stay with him if he wasn't convinced Jesse had it covered. Right now he really wanted to be alone with his frustration. "Just get me home and I'll deal with the rest." His car was still at the firehouse, and he didn't think he could drive it, anyway. One of the guys could bring it over later.

He and Bradens hobbled out to the chief's red truck, the radio still chattering in the dash with all the usual post-incident communication. It had been a small fire, a holiday fish fry spilling over onto a back deck, more smoke and mess than any real damage. Only the deck was old and rickety, as Jesse and his left tibia had soon learned. Those mishaps—the ones that were so infuriatingly avoidable—made Jesse angry even if he didn't end up hurt. If people would just bother to repair things like stairs when they broke, or—better yet—call in someone who knew what they were doing instead of trusting structures to a lethal combination of lumber store supplies and an internet tutorial. As every paramedic in the department knew too well, sometimes "do-it-yourself" turned into "hurt yourself" or "hurt someone else," as tonight well showed.

"It's late." Chief Bradens sighed, looking at the digits on the dashboard clock.

"It's so late it's early," Jesse managed to joke, pointing to the "12:25 a.m." with a strangled smile.

"I hope we get a quiet night from here on in," Chief Bradens said, breaking his own rule. It was a standing joke at the firehouse that hoping aloud for "a quiet night" nearly always guaranteed the opposite. The holiday incidents and short-staffing had really wiped the chief out.

"I hope we get a quiet weekend," Jesse added. "We need a break." He caught his own unintentional joke and laughed, glad to see a weary smile come to the chief's face, as well. "Well, a different kind of break, that is."

They drove to Jesse's apartment in tired silence, listening to the back and forth of the radio chatter slowly die down as the department settled in. The guys on duty would be up for another hour cleaning and restocking before they got to go home to their families. Nights like this were hard under the best of circumstances, much less when they were short of staff, as the GFVFD currently was.

They pulled into the driveway of Jesse's duplex. "I guess it's a good thing you have the first floor." Chief Bradens nodded to the pile of Jesse's turnout gear in the truck's backseat. "I'll take your stuff back to the firehouse for you."

Jesse opened the door and put his good foot—now sporting a paper hospital bootie, since he'd gone in wearing fire boots—on the sidewalk. He angled the crutches out of the truck and stood up. Everything hurt.

Chief came around the car. "You're sure you'll be okay?"

"Fine." He'd keep his cell phone nearby and call

Mom if he needed anything other than the ten hours of sleep he currently craved.

He was fishing in his pocket for his house keys when the beeper went off and they both noticed the radio in the truck spouting a crackle of commands. "Not again," Bradens groaned.

If the chief didn't look so drained and his own body didn't hurt so much, Jesse would have made some crack about Bradens jinxing the night with his hope for quiet. Mostly he just shook his head as the chief hoisted himself onto the passenger seat to grab the radio handset.

"Gotta go. Smoke at 85 Post Avenue."

"Go," Jesse said, turning toward his house. "I'll be fine once I..." He halted, frozen by the facts his tired brain had just this moment absorbed. Then Jesse spun around as fast as his crutches would let him, only to see Bradens's truck speed away, lights blaring as the firehouse siren sent up its second wail of the night.

85 Post Avenue was Charlotte's cottage.

Chapter Sixteen

It no longer felt like home.

That was the single, constant impression Charlotte's Chicago apartment left her with as she rattled around the dull white box of a dwelling. A month ago she'd found the urban apartment dripping with character, but now it felt sadly ordinary. Impersonal, even, despite the fact that it still contained many of her personal belongings. Even the addition of Mo didn't seem to liven up the place. How could a stuffed full apartment feel more vacant than a half-empty cottage?

When she'd pulled out of the driveway in Gordon Falls, she'd doubted the wisdom of that purchase. Now, back in Chicago, she recognized it for what it had become: her home. Sitting in her favorite chair in her Chicago apartment, she still felt uncomfortable and out of place. She wanted to be in Gordon Falls. She wanted to *live* in Gordon Falls for more than just weekends and vacations.

It didn't seem possible—at least not any way that she could see right now. *I want to be there, but there isn't a job for me there. Is there one that I've missed? Lord, why are you opening a door so far away when You've*

*knit my heart to Gordon Falls? Is it because I need to
be away from Jesse? We're not good for each other,
even I can see that, but my heart...*

Charlotte curled up under a lush afghan, welcomed
Mo onto her lap and began to make two lists. One list
held ideas for jobs she could do in Gordon Falls or one
of the neighboring towns—"make do" jobs like marketing for the local hospital or some other company,
office work or finding online work she could do from
home. None of these felt at all exciting or motivating.
The second list held all the arrangements—like finding a moving company or renting a storage facility—
that would be necessary if she went to Vermont. Both
lists left a sour taste in her mouth, and she abandoned
the task in favor of knitting with Mo purring beside her
until she dozed off.

The loud ring of the apartment's landline phone woke
her, clanging from the single receiver in the kitchen. She
bumbled her way to the phone, the alarm of a middle-
of-the-night call fighting with the fatigue of her difficult day. Mo tangled around her feet and she almost
tripped twice. Her answering machine was kicking in
by the time she lifted the receiver. "Hello?"

"Charlotte, what on earth are you doing in Chicago?"

"Melba?" How had her friend even known to call
her here? She hadn't told anyone she was leaving. She'd
planned to call Melba in the morning, but she knew if
she talked to Melba before she left, her friend would
have talked her into staying over. She needed to be farther away from the cottage than the Bradenses' house.
"I decided to come to my apartment. What's wrong?"

Charlotte heard Maria crying in the background.
"I only tried this number because you didn't answer
your cell phone. Charlotte, it's the cottage. One of your

neighbors smelled the smoke and called the fire department."

Charlotte fumbled for her handbag, knocking a tote bag to the ground and sending Mo scurrying back out of the kitchen. "The cottage is on fire?" Panic strangled her breath and sent her thoughts scattering. "The cottage?" she repeated, as if that would help the news sink in.

"I don't know any details yet. No one knew where you were."

She found her cell phone and saw three missed calls—two from Jesse and one from Melba, not to mention multiple texts from both of them. All within the past ten minutes. She'd set the phone to Vibrate during dinner with Jesse and hadn't turned the ringtone back on. "I drove here earlier tonight." Charlotte sat down on one of the tall stools that fronted her kitchen counter. "My house is on fire?" Tears tightened her throat. She couldn't stand to lose something else. She just couldn't.

"Not fully, and the guys have it under control. Clark said it was mostly just smoke but he called me when they didn't find you in the house." Her voice jostled as if she were bouncing Maria to try and soothe the crying child. Charlotte squinted at the cell phone screen to see that it was nearly 1:00 a.m. "I'm so glad you're okay. I've been praying like crazy since I couldn't reach you on your cell phone."

"My house is on fire." She couldn't think of another thing to say. "My house. My cottage." She began stuffing everything back into the tote bag she'd knocked off the counter. "It'll take me hours to get there. Oh, God…" It was a moan of a prayer, a plea for clarity where none existed.

"What if you took the train? Maybe you shouldn't drive."

She couldn't wait for a train. And she surely wouldn't sleep anymore tonight. No, the only thing for it was to head back to Gordon Falls and pray along the way for safe travel. "No, I don't think there's one for hours anyway. I'll call if I need help to stay calm, and I promise I'll pull over if I need to rest." *My house is on fire.* Her brain kept shouting it at her, making it hard to think. She was supposed to be the calm head in a crisis, the problem solver, but none of that felt possible now. "I'll be on my way in ten minutes." She reached into the fridge and stuffed the last three cans of diet cola—a faster caffeine source than waiting for the coffeemaker to brew—into the tote bag. Mo, in a move she knew no other cat owner would probably ever believe, calmly walked into his carrier as if he knew they were getting back into the car. "Call my cell if you learn anything more, okay?"

"I will. Stay safe, Charlotte. The cottage is important, but you're more important than all of that. Don't speed, and call me if you need me. I'll talk to you the whole way in if you need me."

The cell phone buzzed on the counter. Jesse's information lit up the screen.

"Where are you?" his voice shouted over a lot of background noise, including sirens.

"I'm in Chicago. I just talked to Melba."

"Chicago? What are you doing there? I went nuts when they couldn't find you in the house."

There was so much noise behind him. The thought of Jesse standing outside the cottage watching flames eat her house made it harder to fight off the tears. She sat down on the stool. "How bad is it?"

"Not as bad as it could have been. If you had been inside…" Someone barked questions to him and she heard him pull the phone away from his ear and answer, "No, no, I've got her on the phone right now. She's in Chicago. Yeah, I know."

"I'm coming." She was desperate to see the cottage, to know how badly it had been damaged. The 160 or so miles between Chicago and Gordon Falls felt like a thousand right now.

"I would." His voice was unreadable over all that noise. Did he say that because he would have made the same choice? Or was it so bad that she needed to be out there as soon as possible?

"Whoa, Sykes! Ouch! How'd that happen?" She recognized the voice as one of the firemen but couldn't begin to say which one.

"Hey, not now, okay?" came Jesse's quick reply. His voice came close to the phone again. "You be careful driving. Things are under control here, just try and remember that."

What did he say just now? "Jesse, are you okay?"

"I'm fine. Just rattled, that's all. The cottage and everything. Call me when you get to the highway exit." He paused before adding, "I'm glad you're okay. Really glad."

She heard emotion tighten his words and felt her own chest cinch with the awareness. "I should be there sometime before four." She took a minute to breathe before she asked, "Jesse, what aren't you telling me? Is the cottage gone? Just tell me now—I need to know."

"The cottage isn't gone. Looks like mostly smoke and water damage. I didn't get close enough to know anything more than that."

Not close enough? Jesse had been brought in on duty

tonight. Why wasn't he in the crew that went to her house? "But I'd have thought you—"

He cut her off. "Just get here. The longer we talk now, the longer it takes for you to get on the road. I promise, I'll be here when you pull in and I'll answer all your questions then."

"But what—"

"Look, I've got to go. Please promise me you'll drive safely, and you'll pull off if you get sleepy."

She had a gallon of adrenaline running in her veins. "No chance of that. I've got a bunch of Diet Cokes besides." She had to ask. "It's going to be okay, isn't it?"

"Yes."

She wanted him to turn on the charm, to launch into that irresistible persuasion that was his gift, to sweep her up in that bold confidence he had, but really, how could he? A phone conversation in the middle of what might be a disaster couldn't do that. The only thing she knew that could do such a thing was prayer.

"Jesse?"

"Yeah?"

"Pray for me? I know it's not really your thing, but God will hear you anyway, and I'll feel better knowing you're asking Him to keep me safe until I get there." It was a drastic thing to ask, but if this wasn't a time for drastic measures, what was?

"I'll give it a shot."

That was all the foothold she needed. "Okay. Mo and I are on the way."

"Wait…you have the cat with you?" He sounded surprised.

"Evidently he likes car rides."

He pushed out a breath. "I had the guys scouring the neighborhood for the beast. I thought he was a goner, or at the very least ran away." He actually sounded relieved. "Glad to hear he'll live to torment me another day."

Even on the phone, even faced with disaster, he'd managed to pull a smile from her—one just large enough to get her on her way. "See you soon."

Every single bone in his body ached. His leg injury was down to a dull fire thanks to the pain medicine, but Jesse felt the sorry combination of wide awake and exhausted pound through his muscles and thud in his brain.

He should go home. It was feat enough that he'd hobbled all the way here on his crutches—it wasn't that long a walk but still, that had to have been damaging. He should take himself back to his apartment and at least make an effort to get some sleep.

Only he couldn't. He sat on the curb, his splinted leg sticking out in the deserted street atop his crutches in a makeshift attempt at "keeping it elevated," staring at the cottage. He was trying to make the place feel like his cottage, striving to muster up the sense of ownership he'd privately claimed before Charlotte came along. It wouldn't come. This was Charlotte's place, and two things were currently driving him crazy.

One, that he needed to make it Charlotte's perfect place—wonderfully, uniquely hers.

Two, that no matter what he told himself, no matter how "unserious" he claimed to be about that woman, he couldn't stand the thought of her gone.

What had swept through his body when he realized Chief Bradens's radio was crackling out orders for Charlotte's cottage was sharper than fear. It was the bone-deep shock of loss. A loss that wasn't about bricks and shingles, but the woman who'd come to invade his life. He'd told himself it was better to keep things cool, to play their mutual attraction the way the old Jesse would have done. Only he couldn't. She'd done something to him. He'd told himself that his balking over her rental suggestion was just the legendary Sykes ego, a refusal to live in the house over some sore-loser impulse. That would have been a good guess for his personality a month ago. That wasn't it, though—he'd bristled because he hated the idea of the house without Charlotte inside, even temporarily. Somehow he knew—had known since the beginning in a way he couldn't comfortably explain—that she belonged there. Living there instead of her seemed just plain wrong.

Sitting there, feeling something way beyond sidelined, Jesse added two more items to the list of things that were bugging him:

Three, that he couldn't help with the cottage. Normally, Jesse wasn't the kind to rush in toward a fire. There were guys like that, firemen who were nearly obsessively drawn to a crisis, driven by an inner urge to save the day that made ordinary men heroes. He'd never felt that pull—until tonight. It buzzed through him like a ferocious itch that he could only watch from the sidelines. It gave him nothing to do.

Which brought up number four: Charlotte's request that he pray. He could no more help her get here from Chicago than he could march into that cottage, and the sense of helplessness crippled him worse than his leg. The prayer she'd requested was the only thing he could do for her...but he wasn't sure how. He was not a praying man. He wasn't opposed to the idea—he took some comfort in the prayers Chief Bradens or Chad Owens or any of the other firefighters had been known to offer, and he found himself drawn to Charlotte's prayers of grace over their dinners. Still, none of those people had ever directly asked for prayer from him. It was like being told to use a complicated new tool without being given the owner's manual.

Only, was it complicated? Charlotte never made it look like anything more difficult than breathing. Prayer seemed to come to her like singing came to him—something that just flowed out of a person.

Singing.

Jesse searched his memory for a gospel song. He owned nearly every recording Sam Cooke, Aretha Franklin and Bobby Darin ever made, not to mention Ray Charles and Smokey Robinson. One of them had to have a gospel song in there somewhere.

He couldn't remember the title of the song, but his mind recalled Sam Cooke's mournful voice singing, some song about Jesus and consolation. That's what Charlotte needed. And so, after a guilty look around to see if there was anyone who could hear, Jesse began singing the couplets he remembered. Charlotte needed consolation to return to the assurance she'd first proclaimed to him: *God is never late and He's never early; He's always right on time.*

He kept on singing, letting the words soak into his own tangled spirit as he remembered more and more of the lyrics, letting the song undo the knots in his shoulders and the grip in his chest that wouldn't let him breathe. Letting him know that it might not be a bad thing that he felt so bonded to her, and her alone. Slowly, he felt his own words form—not out loud, but like a sigh inside his head, a breath waiting to be exhaled.

"She knows You're there, God. Give her consolation." With something close to a grin, he switched the lyrics so that they were about Charlotte, about her knowing there was consolation. She ought to be halfway by now, closer to Gordon Falls than Chicago. Exhausted as he was, he felt his heart rate pick up at the thought of seeing her soon.

Why was he so frightened of being serious with Charlotte—why be scared of something that had already happened? Getting serious with Charlotte was no longer a proposition; it was a fact. A done deal, whether he was ready for it or not. *I'll sing you home, Charlotte. I'll sing you prayers to bring you home.*

He began improvising a little bit on the melody, stretching it out into long phrases he imagined could cross the miles between himself and Charlotte, bonding them further, reaching into that little blue car as it made its way through the dark. "Charlotte knows You're there. She knows there's consolation."

Do I?

The question from somewhere in the back of his brain startled him so much he bolted upright. *Do I know God is there?*

It was the "know" part that brought him up short. He didn't not believe in God, in the grace of Jesus forgiving sins. He liked to think God was around, working in the world. He'd certainly seen what it did for the lives of people he knew. But did he know, really know in the rock-solid way Charlotte seemed to? The way Charlotte would need him to? The way that offered the consolation he felt himself lacking?

It was then that the title of the song surfaced out of his memory. "Jesus Wash Away My Troubles." It could not be coincidence that of all the gospel songs recorded by all the Motown artists in history, that was the song that came to him on this forlorn street corner in the middle of the night. *You are. You're there.* Jesse felt the astounding sensation of his soul lifting up and settling into place.

He looked around, feeling…feeling what, exactly? *Transformed* was such a dramatic way to put it, but no other word came to mind. He felt lighter. Looser. In possession of a tiny bit of that peace of Charlotte's that pulled him in like a magnet.

This was what made her the way she was. What made her able to ride through life with that indescribable trust that everything would work out in the end, and the courage to leap into situations without hesitation. It was the exact opposite of that drive he had, the one that made him plot and plan and scramble to bend life to his advantage. He'd never trusted that things would work out, because he'd never had anything to trust *in.* But he did now.

Consolation.

He felt consoled. Nothing in tonight's circumstances had changed—the cottage was still a wreck, his leg was still broken, the next six weeks up in the air and all of it beyond his control.

Yesterday's Jesse would be gnawing on his crutches by now. Tonight, he felt absurdly okay with it all.

All of it except the fact that Charlotte was not here. The sting of her absence, the bolt of ice down his back when he thought she might be harmed, the unsettling power of his need for her—those things weren't consolation. They were powerful, a bit wonderful and a great big hunk of terrifying.

Okay, God, this is me, doing the prayer thing. No songs, not someone else's lyrics, just me. And I'm asking You—begging You—to bring her home safe. Keep her head clear enough to drive or smart enough to pull over if she's too tired. I'll wait if I have to. But I figure You already know that I don't want to. Just keep her safe, because I can't. Not from here. That's going to have to be Your department. You get her here and I'll take it from there.

He sat there on the curb in the fading darkness of near dawn, listening to the steady drip of water off the cottage. They hadn't soaked the house, but even a small fire like the one tonight called for a fair amount of water, and firemen never had the luxury of being careful with their hose. He sang all the verses he could remember from "Amazing Grace"—Aretha Franklin had a dynamite ten-minute version on one recording he owned—humming in the parts where he couldn't remember the words. He was segueing into Ray Charles's "O Happy Day," feeling the beginnings of a second wind, when his cell phone rang.

He grabbed it like a lifeline, a gush of "Thank You" surging from his heart when he saw Charlotte's number on the screen. "Charlotte?"

"I just got off the highway. I pulled over on the shoulder on Route 20 to call."

Jesse was glad she was only ten minutes away. She sounded weary. "You're almost here. I'll be up by the floodgates, waiting for you." He wanted to hold her, to give her every ounce of support he could before she saw the cottage.

She guessed his strategy. "That bad, huh?"

"No, not really. It's all fixable from what I can see. But you have to be so tired."

"I am. You must be, too. This was your second fire of the night and you weren't even supposed to be on duty."

Jesse saw no point in giving her the details yet. She'd see the crutches soon enough. "No worries, Miss Taylor. This is what I do. Get back on the road and I'll see you soon."

"Okay." If she hadn't already been crying, she was close to tears. Who wouldn't be in her situation?

Jesse pocketed the phone, picked up his crutches and hobbled toward the floodgates humming "O Happy Day."

Chapter Seventeen

Charlotte worked it out, somewhere west of Rockford. The force of her own idiocy had struck her so hard she'd nearly had to pull over and catch her breath.

She had set her own house on fire.

She'd left the oven on with the paper bag and tin containers of food inside to keep them warm. The greasy nature of Dellio's fries made them downright addictive, but probably also made them something close to kindling if left unsupervised. *Father God, I burned my own house down. How could I have been so foolish?* She wanted to ask Jesse—had tried to, in a roundabout way with her repeated question of "How bad is it?"— but she knew he'd never say. Not while she was driving. He'd save the lecture for when they were face-to-face. *Why did I have to leave right then? Why couldn't I have been sensible and waited until morning or at least until I was calmer?*

Part of her knew the answer: what she felt for Jesse was frightening her. She wasn't ready to love a firefighter. She wasn't ready to accept the life that she saw beat Mom down over the years. Needing someone who could be yanked away from you on a moment's notice?

She didn't think she could handle that. Hadn't she already proved how poorly she handled that? The facts that Jesse didn't have a relationship with God—and seemed to have trouble with relationships in general—were just the icing on the cake.

She wouldn't worry about that right now. Right now she would just get to Gordon Falls, fall exhausted into his arms, thank him for saving her house and praying her safely here, and let him save her for now. The rest of it would have to wait until she could think straight. Charlotte pulled off Route 20 and sighed out loud when she caught sight of the familiar green floodgates that marked the official entrance into Gordon Falls.

The sigh turned into a panicked yelp when her headlights shone on Jesse. He was standing on a pair of crutches with a bandage over one eyebrow, and a splint on one leg.

He'd been hurt. And he hadn't told her. Had he been injured fighting the fire at her cottage? A dozen thoughts slammed together in her head as she threw open the car door and raced up to him.

"You're okay!" He reached out to her as much as the crutches would allow.

"You're not!" As much as she wanted to melt into his arms and cry buckets of tired tears, the shock of seeing him injured wedged between them. "You're hurt. What happened? Why didn't you tell me?" It was as if the omission of that detail let loose a deluge of her own panic, and everything she'd been holding in check the entire drive came gushing out of her in a choking wave of sobs.

"Hey." He tried to grab her but she darted out of his grasp. "Hey, I'm okay. I didn't think you needed the extra stress of the news on the drive."

She noticed the bloody bandage on his leg above the splint and felt a bit dizzy. In her mind she heard her mother yelling at her father. The one night he'd been seriously injured—a stab wound in his shoulder—he'd simply waltzed in the door with his arm in a sling and Mom had gone through the roof. Now she knew how that felt. "You were hurt and you didn't tell me? You were hurt fighting the fire *at my cottage* and you didn't think I could handle knowing? So it's bad enough that I started the fire, why add to my guilt? Is that what you think of me?" Some part of her knew she was being unreasonable but she couldn't stop the spiral of panic and guilt that wrapped itself around her.

Jesse managed to grab her arm, the force of his grasp startling her out of the tailspin. "Look at me. Charlotte, *look at me.*" His eyes were fierce, but in a protective way. He pulled her toward him. "I am fine." He spoke the words slowly, clear and close. Charlotte latched on to them like an anchor line. "I'm hurt, yes, but I'm going to be okay. We're both going to be okay."

She didn't see how any of this was going to be anything close to okay. She started to shake her head, but Jesse tugged her closer, crutches still under both arms, and held her close.

"You're here. You're safe. That's what matters." He let the crutches fall against the side of her car, holding her face in his hands. "I went nuts when I realized it was your house. I would have run there in my bare feet if it weren't for this." He wobbled a bit, standing on one leg, and she helped him hop over and sit on the hood. "When they couldn't find you…"

His words struck her. "You were hurt at the first fire?" It was still awful, but the weight on her chest eased up a bit. She looked at his leg. "What happened?"

"I tripped and fell into a porch railing. The railing was in bad shape, so it gave way and I went down. Kind of hard."

Only Jesse would make light of something like that. "And…"

"Broken tibia and sixteen stitches."

She put her hands to her mouth. "Oh, wow. That's bad."

"Well, it's not the 'put some dirt on it and walk it off' kind of thing, but I'll be all right." His hands came up to her hair. "I was worried about you. I was close to banging down your cousin JJ's door and getting one of those corporate helicopters her husband uses rather than forcing you to make that drive."

She knew Jesse would have, too. She hadn't imagined what had sprung up between them; it was real. "Alex doesn't run a huge corporation anymore, you know that."

"I just kept thinking about you all alone on that dark highway, tired and scared. For a guy's first prayer you sure picked a doozy. I'd say 'baptism by fire,' but I think that would be in poor taste."

Charlotte touched the bandage over his eye. His eyes. He could never fake what was in his eyes right now. It was no trick of entertainment; it was deep, true care. "So you did pray?"

"Of course. You asked me to. I couldn't work out how at first, so I just started singing whatever gospel song I could remember. It got easier after that. I just tried to believe as much as I know you do, hoping it would rub off."

"Did it?"

The warmth in his eyes ignited further, and she felt his hands tighten around her waist as she stood next to him beside the car. "Yeah, it did. I couldn't help you from where I was, but I began to feel like God could. Like He would." He looked down and shook his head. "I don't know how to explain it, really."

She lifted his chin to meet her eyes. That wasn't just warmth or care, it was peace. "No explanation needed. I get it. And I'm glad." The peace that had momentarily abandoned her—or had she abandoned it?—returned bit by bit. She allowed the strength of his embrace to seep into her, felt his head tilt to touch the top of hers and leave a handful of tender kisses there. Real. True. Trustworthy.

"You may not be so glad in a few minutes. The cottage is a mess. It's still there, it didn't burn, but there's a lot of damage."

She cringed. Her beautiful cottage—undone by a burger and fries with a side of stupidity. "I started it. Oh, Jesse, the fire is my fault. The oven…"

He tightened his grip on her. "I know. Clark told me they found the Dellio's tin in the oven. Or what's left of the oven." He put his face close to hers. "We'll get through it. Just…"

"Just what?"

His entire face changed, the fierceness leaving to reveal a heart-stopping tenderness. "Just don't leave. Don't go to Vermont, Charlotte. I don't want you to go. You belong here. You belong with me. You know you do, don't you?"

She knew how much it cost him to admit that, to make the request, and the last piece of her heart broke open for this incredible man. "I want to, but how?"

"I don't know yet. But if God is never late and He's never early, then maybe He's never wrong. I'm pretty new at this, but you told me yourself you felt like God led you here. It's got to still be true. We'll just have to figure out how to trust that."

Jesse's work with the GFVFD put him in the position of dealing with friends and neighbors after a fire, so he should have been used to this. None of that explained how his heart drummed against his ribs as he rode in Charlotte's little blue car, crutches banging against his shoulders, frustrated that he was forced to let her drive.

The damage on the outside wasn't especially visible in the predawn light, though there were *some* signs. The loose front railing had given way when knocked by one of the firefighters, and it lay propped up against the side of the cottage. The bushes Charlotte had just trimmed after months of neglect were trampled, and there were divots and gashes in the front lawn, scraggly as it was.

He caught her gaze as she turned off the ignition in the driveway. "See, it's still here. Not even a window broken. You should realize how fortunate you are." He wanted to reassure her, bolster her up before she saw the inside. He'd not been in there yet, but he knew what to expect. He dreaded watching her eyes take in the overwhelming sooty blackness he knew would cover her home.

"Yeah, I know." She said the words for his benefit, her tone hollow with disbelief.

He grabbed her hand, needing to make her understand. "Your neighbor called when she heard your smoke detectors go off and she didn't see any lights come on in the house. If it had become fully involved in open flames, I don't think you'd have much of a cottage left." He tried to put it into the terms that would mean the most to her. "You're blessed, Charlotte. It could have been so much worse."

Her grip on his hand tightened. "You put those smoke detectors in for me."

"And boy, am I glad." There was no way he was going to let her sleep in that house without the best smoke detectors he could get. It was the one extravagance he endorsed without a hint of guilt. He couldn't help drawing the connection between that urge and her current safety. He knew Charlotte wouldn't call that coincidence, and it was starting to sink in that it wasn't. He'd been placed in Charlotte's life right at this time. *God is never late, and He's never early; He's always right on time.* "Come on, let's get the first look over with. It gets better after that."

She hesitated, one hand still white-knuckled on the steering wheel. "What's in there?"

"I don't know. I haven't been in yet."

"Yes, but you know what to expect. Tell me what I'm going to find."

Jesse took a deep breath. Perhaps this was the least he could do—lessen the sensory shock so that it didn't hit her like a brick wall. He pulled her hand into his lap and stroked it softly while he kept his tone low and calm. "It will smell bad—at least for now. It's good that you don't have a lot of furniture in there yet." He thought of the little plaid chair where he'd imagined resting his leg. "Most of the textiles might need to go or be professionally cleaned."

"All my yarn and fabrics are still in Chicago. And my china, too—well, most of it." Her grappling for positives unwound his heart.

"Yep, that's good. Most of the kitchen will be covered in black soot and probably some whitish powder from the extinguishing agent. Probably some of the dining room and hallway, too. None of the windows are broken, so that's good, too."

"My new sink and faucet are goners, aren't they?"

"Maybe, maybe not." He gave her hand a final squeeze before he let go and opened the car door. "There's only one way to find out." When she winced, he added, "I'll be right beside you, Charlotte. Now and all the way through this."

Before he could get himself out of the car, Charlotte grabbed his shoulder and gave him a tender kiss. If there had been any resistance left in him, the need he felt in that kiss dissolved the last trace. The small, insistent longing to make her happy swelled into a consuming urge. He returned her kiss as if he were sealing a promise. *I will see you through this. I will stand by you.*

"Thank you," she said, their foreheads still touching.

He started to say, "You're welcome," but the words weren't near adequate. Instead, he kissed her again, hoping his touch spoke more. "Okay." He forced a grin and a wink. "Enough necking in the driveway. Let's get the hard part over with."

Her hands were shaking as she pulled aside the yellow tape that held the door shut. They'd had to break down the door. "Oh well, I was thinking about a new front door anyway."

"That's the spirit. Ready?"

"No." She managed the smallest slip of a smile, a weak and wobbly thing that still looked breathtaking on her.

"Want me to go first?"

She pushed back her shoulders and raised her chin. "No. I can do this."

You can. I know you can. In that moment, Jesse knew she'd come through this even stronger. Chief Bradens said he could always tell which people would beat the fire, and which people would let the fire beat them. In this case, Jesse could see it, too. Charlotte wouldn't let this keep her down for long. Jesse felt his heart slip from his grasp as she stepped across the threshold.

The acrid scent of smoke hit them with a force that was almost physical as he followed her into the house. Her hands went up to her face. "Oh, Lord, help me." It wasn't a casual expression—it was a heartfelt plea to heaven. Jesse, to his own surprise, felt a similar plea launch up from his own heart—*Help me help her.*

The front hallway and living room weren't as bad as they could have been. Thin black film covered everything, but he'd seen far worse. In the gray-pink light of dawn, it was as if the room had been poorly erased; everything blended together in a smudge of colorless dust. He made his way over to the windows and began opening them up. He'd go through the house with Charlotte and open every working window until the worst of the smell had eased up a bit. It would feel like progress to her, and he knew all she really needed was a first foothold.

He heard a whimper and turned to find her staring at the plaid chair, now damp and smudged with soot. He could tell her something optimistic, but he owed her the respect of honesty. "You'll have to trash it. I'm sorry."

She hugged her elbows and shrugged. "It was so perfect." It was true. She'd grown ridiculously attached to that chair ever since the day she'd brought it home, half hanging out of the hatch of the tiny blue car. It had made him wonder how it hadn't fallen out on the way home and why she hadn't asked him to pick it up in his truck, which would have held four such chairs easily.

"You'll find another perfect one. Maybe a pair this

time." He wanted to swallow the words back—a pair?—what kind of dorky misplaced romantic comment was that?

Opening two more windows, Jesse made his way to the kitchen, taking care not to slip on anything with his crutches. He was due back at the hospital in three hours, where he would have to explain why he had not, in fact, done anything close to "take it easy and keep it elevated." The last dose of painkillers had worn off and his leg was throbbing.

"Oh." Charlotte's word was more of a gasp. "It's ruined. It's all ruined."

Jesse went over to one of the blackened cabinets, which looked like someone had set a dozen cans of black spray paint on the stove and triggered them in every direction. The new stove was a total loss, as were the cabinets directly above and around them. He had kissed her up against one of those cabinets. Every scorched corner of the room held a memory for him.

Even more so for her. Charlotte was pacing around the room, hands outstretched as if she needed to touch everything but couldn't bring herself to do so. "Everything is covered in black."

He opened one of the cabinets, wanting to show her one thing that hadn't been blackened. The interior wasn't scorched, but the plastic containers inside were slumped into melted, distorted forms. Her teapot lay in pieces on the far corner of the kitchen floor. The mason jar that had held his flowers the first time he'd brought them for her lay cracked with a big chip out of the top. One chair lay sideways on the floor, a leg bent in on itself and smeared in black. Footprints and smudge marks covered the once cheery lemon-colored linoleum floor she'd wanted so badly to keep.

"I did this." She stood in the center of the room, losing her battle to the returning tears she'd been trying so hard to fight off since the floodgates. "I'm so stupid to have done this."

She wouldn't hear any argument he might make right now. So Jesse did the only thing there was to do. He leaned against the counter for support, and pulled her to him. He let her cry it out, holding her tight and singing "Jesus Wash Away My Troubles," with his eyes closed and his heart wide open.

Chapter Eighteen

"Charlotte! Charlotte, where are you in here?" Melba's shocked voice called from the hallway.

"Kitchen," Charlotte called out, then sniffed and wiped her eyes with the corner of the zip-up sweatshirt she'd been wearing. Already it had black streaks on it, the fabric beginning to give off the tang of soot and smoke. Her eyes stung from more than the onslaught of tears.

"Look at this place. Thank heavens you're safe." Melba's hug somehow brought everything into full reality, making Charlotte instantly exhausted. She needed to sit down but didn't have a single clean spot to do so. "Clark told me it wasn't as bad as it could have been, but it looks awful enough to me."

Jesse seemed to sense her weariness. "Let's go out onto the back porch. There's still a lot of smoke and soot in here, and I could use a dose of fresh air."

"And Mo. He's yowling in the car, you know."

"I forgot about Mo!" Charlotte rushed to the car to find a disgruntled Mo protesting his neglect from the backseat. In the emotion of the past hour, she'd not even remembered he was there. She pulled him from the car—

rier, keeping one hand on his collar. "Oh, big guy, this isn't a place for you to be inside right now. We'll get you set up in a little while, but I need you to stay put." Guilt over Mo piled on top of her grief and stress over the house. "This isn't much of a new home, is it? It'll get better, I promise." She found some strong yarn in one of the bags in her trunk and tied it to Mo's collar. "The back porch is the best I can do for you right now. Be nice to Jesse, okay? He's done a lot for us and he even went looking for you."

She walked around the side of the house, wincing at the dark streaks around the kitchen window and wondering if they would wash off or if she'd have to repaint.

She walked up the back porch steps, Mo still in her arms, to find Melba had pushed open the back door and propped it wide with a sooty box of books. Jesse had maneuvered himself into one of the porch's bistro chairs. He looked exhausted and uncomfortable.

"Clark told me you were hurt in the first fire," Melba was saying to Jesse, as Charlotte practically fell into the other chair and settled Mo on her lap. "It's broken, huh?"

Jesse nodded, one eye on Mo. His regard toward the animal had softened a bit. Charlotte was so touched that he'd gone in search of "the little beast" before he knew Mo was with her in Chicago.

Melba settled herself on the porch steps. "I was worried sick, Charlotte. I wished you'd called me when you got into town."

Charlotte leaned back in the chair, fatigue growing stronger with every minute. "You were asleep. You had Maria to tend to. I knew Jesse was waiting." Charlotte yawned. She'd been up for almost twenty-four hours now, and it was taking its toll.

Within seconds, Melba had her "mother face" on. "Have either of you slept at all?"

"Not exactly." Jesse yawned the words, although they had more of a wince quality to them. He hadn't said anything about the pain he was in, but it was obvious he hurt. Badly. The bandage on his leg was starting to grow pink at the center.

Melba stared at Jesse's bandage and splint as well, coming to the same conclusion. "Clark's dropping Maria off with JJ and Alex. He'll be here in ten minutes. Charlotte, you're coming home to shower and sleep at our house while Clark takes you to your apartment to do the same, Jesse. Clark's dad is skipping church to come pick you up for your hospital appointment at ten-thirty and deliver you back home. I should tell you, Chief George has orders from Clark to tie you to your couch if that's what it takes." Melba's father-in-law was fire chief before his son took over the job, and Charlotte knew George now served as an unofficial guardian of sorts to the firehouse. Jesse could use that kind of support right now.

"I don't think I have the strength to argue with that," Jesse said, shifting his weight tenderly. "Charlotte needs to sleep."

"So do you," Charlotte added, a surge of gratitude for all Jesse had done in the past hours welling up and threatening a new bout of tears. "You've probably done a million bad things to that leg in the last eight hours."

"I haven't exactly kept it rested and elevated, if that's what you mean." He held Charlotte's eyes for a long moment. "I had other priorities."

"These firemen," Melba chided. "They think they're invincible." She walked over and stood over Jesse. "Where are your pain meds? Your antibiotics?" She was on full mother alert now. Charlotte had seen it when Melba was caring for her ailing father. It was not wise to mess with Melba when she was in caregiving mode.

"Back at the apartment." He had the good sense to look sheepish, like a kid caught skipping his chores.

"A fat lot of good they're doing you back there."

"Yes, I hurt. Everything hurts. I need my medications. I'll go home with Chief and I'll keep my doctor's appointment—after some sleep. Okay, Mom?" His half-exaggerated pout told Charlotte he was nearing the end of his good humor, and so was she.

"It isn't like we can do anything right now except air the house out anyway." Melba planted her hands on her hips. "I'm going to go see how many windows I can get open."

"You'll need my help on some of those." Jesse made to rise but Melba pushed him back down.

"I'll do just fine. And what I can't get open, Clark will. You sit tight, both of you." She fished around in her handbag until she produced a pair of granola bars. "Eat something." Then she disappeared back into the house, a few expressions of her dismay echoing from the mudroom and kitchen.

Jesse sighed and tore open the wrapper. "She's a total mom now. Like someone threw a switch inside her, you know?"

"She's always been the caregiving type. It's why she came here to take care of her dad." Charlotte tied the other end of Mo's yarn leash to the porch railing and went over to kneel at Jesse's feet. "How are you, really?"

Mo, after giving Charlotte a "you gotta be kidding me" glare and swatting once at his makeshift leash, sauntered over to brush against Jesse's good leg. With a small "harumph," Jesse reached down and ran one hand over the cat's fat back. They were making friends after all. "I wasn't kidding. I hurt. Everywhere, it seems."

Charlotte noticed a bruise on his forearm and some scrapes on his knuckles. The risks of what he did clashed with the care she felt for him. It was an awful tug-of-war inside her, and she was too tired to endure it. She couldn't think of anything to say other than "I'm sorry."

He ducked his head down to meet her eyes. "It's not your fault."

It was the wrong thing to say. Tears welled up in her eyes and she nodded back toward the house. "Oh, this most definitely is my fault."

"The usefulness of that debate right now aside, my leg is not your fault. Firemen get hurt. It comes with the territory. Always has."

And that was the problem, wasn't it? "Have you been hurt before?"

She watched Jesse start to give her some wisecrack answer, then stop himself in favor of the honest truth. She was glad he didn't try to brush this matter off—it was important. "Not this badly. Mostly cuts and bruises. I chipped a tooth once. Usually I'm a pretty careful guy."

"What happened, then?"

A hint of a smile reached the corners of his eyes. "I had an argument with someone I care about. Something about Vermont, but it's all kind of fuzzy right now." He leaned down toward her. "I meant what I said, Charlotte. I don't want you to go. I know it's not my decision and I can't tell you what to do, but I don't want you to go to Vermont. Even for a year. Even for a month."

Charlotte touched the bandage, the splint. "I don't know if I can do this. I told myself I'd never do this."

"I told myself I'd never do church, but I prayed so hard tonight I thought God Himself would drop His jaw in surprise. Maybe it's not as hard as we think."

Charlotte let her head fall on Jesse's lap, feeling Mo curl up beside her. "Maybe it's harder. Maybe we're kidding ourselves."

She felt Jesse stroke her hair. "I'm not saying God allowed your house to burn, but what if He knew it would take something this drastic to get us together?"

She angled her head up to look at him. "Are we together?"

"That depends on whether or not you need to go to Vermont." There was a cautious pleading in his eyes that broke Charlotte's heart wide open.

"I don't know," she admitted. "I want to stay here, but I don't know if I can."

"We can find a way. I believe that."

She let his confidence bolster her own. "I believe you."

Clark's voice came from the mudroom doorway. "Okay, kids, it's time for bed."

Jesse frowned. "And *he's* become a total dad."

Jesse held up his hand as he sat on the exam table. "Don't start on me, please. Chief George has been laying into me for the last twenty minutes." Chief George hadn't been fire chief for over a year now since his son Clark took over, but no one had ever stopped calling him by that name.

Dr. Craig crossed his arms over his chest. "Let's just say I don't agree with your definition of 'keeping off it.' You didn't help yourself last night."

"Well, no." George, after his brisk lecture, had been amazingly supportive once Jesse opened up about what happened to him in the heart sense, and yes, in the soul sense—although it felt weird to talk about his own soul—during that long wait on the curb outside of Charlotte's cottage. Truth be told, Jesse was still grasping for ways to understand what had happened last night and this morning, much less explain it. He just knew his life had made an important turn.

He was glad Chief George seemed to understand. The former chief had unofficially adopted every single guy in the firehouse—and many of the married ones. The GFVFD was his family, even though he was only Clark's actual father. More than once in the conversation, Jesse had been stung by the thought of what his life might have been like if he'd had a father as supportive as George Bradens. He was pretty sure his own dad loved him; it was just that Dad's love came with so many requirements before it was paired with approval. Jesse always felt as if he had to earn his father's affections, whereas George seemed to be so generous in giving his—even if it came with a lecture or two.

"He didn't help himself at all, medically," George asserted, placing a fatherly hand on Jesse's shoulder. "But let's simply say the evening evened out." George offered a wink. It made Jesse wonder if Clark had sent his dad for this task by convenience or by design. He'd tried to give Clark a sense of what the night had been for him, but he was far too tired to make much sense. Explanations and talent-show serenades aside, Jesse was pretty sure Clark could have been fast asleep and still have sensed the bond now strung between himself and Charlotte.

And what exactly was that bond? That song at the talent show had shown him Charlotte was different from any other woman. Even as he'd taken steps not to single her out, his gut was telling him he wanted to single her out. *Exclusive.* That wasn't a term Jesse had ever cared to apply to women before Charlotte. Did that mean he was in love with her? Maybe. Whatever it was, Jesse knew it was powerful and worth whatever last night had cost him. That didn't change the worry in the pit of his stomach at the doctor's scowl. His leg looked awful and felt terrible.

"It's gonna be okay, right, Doc? I mean, I didn't do any real harm." He knew he was fishing for reassurance.

Dr. Craig seemed in no hurry to give it. "I can't say for sure. You broke it on an angle. Any weight you put on it last night could have shifted the bones and made things worse. How's your pain today?"

He didn't want to admit how badly it hurt. "Well…"

"Son," George cut in, "there are three people you should never hedge your answers to, ever. One's your lawyer and the other's your doctor."

"And the third?" Jesse felt the punch line of a bad joke coming on.

"Yourself."

Okay, that wasn't so funny. "All right, it hurts a lot. The medicine takes it down to a dull roar, but I'm dying before I get to the next dose. And…I sort of skipped a dose overnight. I was out at the fire site and I left all the prescriptions back at my apartment."

Was the pop-eyed shock from the doctor really necessary? "You went to a fire scene last night?" His face went from surprise to annoyance to dismissal in a matter of seconds. "You hero types make my job a lot harder than it needs to be."

"I'd classify last night as extenuating circumstances, if that helps," George cut in. "Jesse did what he had to do. We can't change that, so can we just move on from what we've got here?"

It seemed as though Dr. Craig dropped any pretense of gentleness as he bent to examine Jesse's throbbing shin more closely. His leg had turned a startling shade of purple, among other pessimistic medical appearances, and Jesse fought the nagging sense that the night had cost him far more than he realized. Personally and professionally, he could take an enormous hit here.

"We'll need another set of X-rays to see if the bone has shifted, but given how it looks—" the doctor doubled his scowl "—and from what you've told me, I'd say we're looking at surgery. Maybe even pins or a plate."

Jesse slumped back against the examining table, all his bleary-eyed wonder at last night giving way to a rising dread. "It's just a break. People break their legs all the time."

"It's a bad break that you put weight on—all night long, evidently. I've half a mind to schedule you for surgery just so I can admit you right now." Straightening up, the doctor put his glasses back in his lab coat pocket. "Mr. Sykes, would your cooperation be too much to ask for here?"

"I'll be a good patient from here on in, Doc. I promise." He folded his hands on his lap, trying to look penitent. "Where do we go from here?"

Dr. Craig picked up a chart and began writing. "I can't cast you—the swelling hasn't gone down sufficiently. I'm sending you for X-rays. We'll change the dressing on that wound and then see what the X-rays tell us. You might get lucky, but I think you should be prepared for the possibility of surgery tomorrow morning." He put the brace back on, which made Jesse wince. "When was your last dose of painkillers?"

Jesse had yearned to swallow a double dose the moment he woke up from his nap earlier. The twenty minutes it took for the stuff to kick in felt almost longer than the wait for Charlotte to pull into Gordon Falls last night. This morning. Had it all really just happened? He felt as if he'd lived a year in the space of those hours. "Six this morning. I'm due. Believe me, I'm due."

George padded the pocket of his windbreaker. "I've got 'em right here."

"I'll have the nursing assistant bring you some water when she comes in to change the bandage. You'll want them—the boys in radiology aren't known for their tender touch." He closed the chart. "I'll see you back here afterward and we'll talk about next steps."

"Okay, Doc." Jesse tried to look cooperative and hopeful, but it was hard with his leg screaming at him. In five minutes he'd down those capsules without water if that nurse hadn't shown up yet. The pain—and his doubts—were beginning to make it hard to keep his trademark humor.

As the examining room door closed, George pulled his cell phone from his pocket and began tapping with youthful speed. "Time to call the cavalry." The former chief had taken to texting with enthusiasm; he sent more "Gexts"—as the firehouse had come to call the numerous electronic check-ins the man was prone to send— than most of the teenagers Jesse knew.

"Huh?"

"Church."

He'd heard stories about the ladies of GFCC swooping in to care for people, but he wasn't sure casseroles were what he needed right now. "You don't need to do that."

George kept typing. "Oh, yes, I do. We need to pray

that leg into cooperation. We want those X-rays to show you haven't hurt yourself further by what you did last night. That's going to take prayer."

This was foreign territory. People praying for him? Him praying for himself? For Charlotte? The world had tilted in new directions overnight, and Jesse still wasn't quite sure how to take it all in. "Um…okay…I guess." It probably was going to take divine intervention to keep him off the operating table. "I'll be okay, though, if I have to go under." He rubbed his eyes, reaching for a way to explain his foggy thoughts. He looked at George. "I mean, it was worth it."

One end of George's mouth turned up in a knowing grin. "I agree. But I'm still lighting up the prayer chain for that leg of yours. After all, you're part of the church now."

He was part of a church. Jesse waited for that to feel odd, or forced, but it just sort of sank into his chest like a deep breath. "I guess I am. Not such a bad thing, is it?"

George's grin turned into a wide smile that took over the old man's entire features. "Best thing there is."

Chapter Nineteen

Charlotte found her way to the kitchen, hoping for a cup of steaming tea to face what was left of the day.

"Hey there." Melba looked up from feeding Maria. "They prayed for both you and Jesse at service this morning. Feeling better?"

Charlotte walked over to the sink and began filling the kettle. Did she even have a teakettle at the cottage anymore? What kind of person has a life that destroys two teakettles in so short a time? "Not really. Less exhausted, but now I feel like I have twice as many thoughts slamming through my head." She sat down at the table opposite Melba and Maria. They looked so peaceful and happy.

"You'll be okay, Charlotte. You know that, don't you?"

She ran her hands through her hair. Even with a long hot shower, Charlotte felt as though she still smelled of smoke. "It's a little hard to see today."

"Maybe today's not a good judge of everything. Clark says it takes two days for the shock to wear off, longer for some people." She looked at Charlotte with such warmth in her eyes. "You can stay here for as long as you need to. Really."

Charlotte knew she meant it, but Melba and Clark had played host to her long enough. She didn't want to stay any longer than absolutely necessary. They deserved to be a family on their own again. "Thanks. I know I need a few days to get my feet underneath me, but I've still got my place in Chicago."

That wiped the warmth from Melba's eyes. "I hate the thought of you being back there. I hate the idea of you going to Vermont even more. I know it's selfish of me, but I really feel like you belong here. Even with everything that's happened."

Charlotte didn't have an answer. Her brain felt far too clouded to think. She was grateful the kettle's whistle gave her something to fill the silence.

Melba settled Maria on her shoulder and began patting the baby's back to burp her. "You want to tell me what happened with Jesse last night? And don't say nothing, because it's all over both of your faces, not to mention what Clark told me last night."

Turning to her friend, Charlotte asked, "What did Clark tell you?"

"That Jesse went crazy with worry when the call came and they realized it was your cottage. That he ignored the doctor's orders and walked to the scene because Clark had already left. That he was frantic to know you were okay, and it was all the guys could do to keep him from trying to help."

Mo, who had thankfully made fast friends with Melba's cat, Pinocchio, darted into the room to weave his way around Charlotte's legs as she set the tea to steeping.

"And that he hobbled around the neighborhood calling for Mo when no one was found in the house." Melba stood up and walked over to Charlotte. "That man has it bad for you. And you have it bad for him."

"It's just that after the display at the talent show, and all he said about not wanting to get serious with any one woman—well, he didn't come right out and say that, but it wasn't hard to guess—I didn't know if I could trust his charm. I don't want to be dazzled."

"But he's gotten to you, and he cares about you—a lot, obviously. I know it's not perfect, but do you really want to walk away from that?"

"*And* he's a firefighter. I know that's okay for you, but—"

"And then there's the whole faith thing, and that's big, too—especially now that he's made the first steps, from what I've heard."

"That's just it. Those things are sort of working themselves out. And for the first part...what he told me, the way he treated me last night at the fire, you can't fake that. His heart is true, I know that now. Only, is that really enough?" She told Melba the entire story of Jesse's night, how he'd come to terms with the God she knew had been pursuing him since the night of the talent show. "It wasn't really God Jesse was resisting, it was his preconceptions of church and judgment. His father's been putting him down for years. That made it hard for him to grasp a Father who loves unconditionally, you know?" She remembered him holding her in the destroyed kitchen, singing a gospel song she'd never heard before but now felt engraved on her heart. What could be a deeper truth than that? "He has such a huge heart, Melba. It's been aching for grace for so long."

Melba started to get mugs down from the cabinet,

only to stop and look straight at Charlotte. "Do you think you're in love with him?"

Charlotte leaned against the counter, squinting her eyes shut for a moment. "Shouldn't I *know* if I'm in love with him?"

"I think it slams some people clearly like that, but I think more often it is something that slowly takes shape. Like knitting with a striped yarn—sometimes you don't see what it really looks like until you get further along."

"The attraction is certainly there." Charlotte thought of the head-spinning serenade that had made it hard to breathe back at the talent show. "The man knows how to sweep me off my feet, Melba, but just because he can doesn't make him the right man for me." She poured the tea into the pair of mugs Melba set on the counter. "You know how impulsive I am. Vermont was going to give me the space to think about this. Maybe it still should."

"Are you running to or running from?"

"What?"

"It's something Clark always says. About jogging or even guys at a fire. People rarely get hurt running to something, but they often injure themselves running *from* something. If you go to Vermont, are you running to what could be a good job or running away from what could be a good man?"

Melba had managed to boil the whole storm of Charlotte's thoughts down to one piercing question. Was she really enthused about Borroughs's offer, or was it just an escape from facing the scary prospect of loving a man who risked his life for others? "I don't know. I don't even know how to figure it out."

"Maybe that's why you ought to talk to Abby Reed this afternoon. She's coming by in an hour if you're feeling up to it."

"Abby?" Abby had a reputation as a notorious match-maker. If she'd taken Jesse on as her newest project, Charlotte didn't see how she'd lend any clarity to the situation. "What's she got to do with any of this?"

Melba's smile was sweet but a little secretive. "I think you'd better hear that from Abby herself. I'm going to go put Maria down for her nap. Why don't you go sit on the deck and just relax for a while. It's a beautiful day, and you need all the doses of fresh air you can get."

The next thing Charlotte knew, someone was gently tapping her on the shoulder as she lay slouched in one of Melba's back deck lounge chairs. She forced her eyes open. "I must have dozed off."

"I'll bet you needed a nap." Abby Reed sat down on the chair opposite Charlotte, a kind smile on her face and a bag of chocolate-covered caramels in her hands. "I know chocolate doesn't make everything better, but it makes most things better."

Charlotte sat up and accepted the bag, reaching in for one of the sweets. "I guess it pays to be good friends with the candy lady."

"Jeannie wants to help in any way she can. She's been through a fire, too, you know. She lost everything a while back, and she knows how it can pull the rug out from underneath you."

"I keep trying to remember I haven't lost everything, but it still feels like I have. There's soot over every-thing." She smoothed her hair out, thinking she prob-ably looked like a mess today. "The fire was my fault, you know—food that I left in the oven and forgot about. I've made such a mess of things with my own stupid-ity. I used to think of myself as such a clever person."

"You're still a clever person. You're just a clever person in a tight spot. We've all been there. Gordon Falls is full of people who are great helps in tight spots."

Charlotte knew that. She could feel the pull of Gordon Falls's tight-knit community calling to her even before her house filled with smoke. "I'm not going to end up with a refrigerator full of church-lady casseroles, am I?" She winced. "I don't think I even have a working fridge anymore, much less a stove to heat them in."

Abby laughed. "You might. GFCC is good at crisis management with food. It's a universal church thing, I think. Jeannie will tell you one of the blessings of a crisis is all the help that comes to your side. I know it may not feel like it this morning, but I'm sure you'll come out of this fine."

"I'm not so sure."

"Then I'd have another caramel if I were you."

No one had to twist Charlotte's arm. When the delicious, sticky confection allowed her to talk again, she prompted, "Melba said you had something you wanted to talk to me about?"

Abby settled her hands on her lap. "I've had an idea for a while now, and before last night I was going to wait until the fall. Now I think I shouldn't wait. Charlotte, I'd like to ask you to consider running a new shop for me. I want to expand the store to open a full yarn and fabric shop in the space next to mine. I'm looking to knock the wall out between the stores and create two connected spaces—one dedicated to gifts and art, the other for crafting. Only I can't run the both of them—really, I don't want to. When Ben finally moves out, I don't want to spend my newly earned free time behind a cash register or in a stock room."

Charlotte's brain struggled to comprehend what she

was hearing. "You want me to work for you? Open up a yarn shop next to your store?"

"I'd thought of it more as a partnership, but that was further down the road. I figure that's a bit much to take on right now. I'd mentioned it to Melba a while ago— just as an inkling I'd had when you first said something about job hunting at the knitting group—but when she told at church this morning that you were considering going to New Hampshire or wherever it was, I had a long talk with God about whether I might need to speed up my time frame."

"Vermont," Charlotte clarified, and then thought that was a stupid thing to say. She blinked and ran her hands down her face, reaching for a focus that she couldn't quite attain. "Not that it matters." She straightened up, planting her feet on the ground as if that would help. "You're serious? You're offering me a job? Here?"

"There are probably lots of details to iron out, but yes. I want you to know you have an option to stay here if you want to. I'm not at all sure I can match whatever you were making at Monarch, but—"

"I want to stay here," Charlotte cut in. She blinked again. "I don't think I even realized how much until just this moment. I don't want to go to Vermont." She held Abby's gaze, feeling a bit dizzy. "Thank you. I'm sure we can figure something out."

Abby's smile told Charlotte this was no pity offer, this was God at work, moving things to His perfect timing. "I'm sure, too. After all, we both know you are a very clever person."

Charlotte was sitting on his front steps by the time George pulled into Jesse's driveway. Jesse was glad to see a little more of the old Charlotte back in her eyes. That smile did more for him than all those painkillers.

"Well now, look who's waiting to take over nurse duties," George teased as he pulled the crutches out of his backseat while Jesse opened the passenger door. "Toss me your keys, son, and I'll get your front door open while you say hello to the lady."

Charlotte ran a hand down Jesse's cheek, and he felt his whole body settle at her touch. "Hello, you."

He leaned up and gave her a small but soft kiss to her cheek. She smelled just-showered; clean and flowery. It was like fresh air compared to the disinfectant-soaked doctors' rooms. "Hello to you, too." He stood up and tilted his head close to hers, closing his eyes and stealing another breath. "You smell amazing, do you know that?"

He felt her smile against his cheek. "Flattery just might get you better nursing care." She pulled away to eye him. "How'd it go?"

He'd have to tell her sometime, might as well get it over with on the front sidewalk. "Not well."

Alarm darkened her features. "What do you mean?"

He started making his way carefully to the front door. "I messed my leg up pretty badly. I'm going to need surgery. I have to be at the hospital tomorrow morning at some cruel hour." He tried to keep the anger out of his voice, but her eyes told him he hadn't been successful. George's "prayer warriors," as he called them, hadn't won this particular battle.

"Surgery? Oh, Jesse."

Somehow the worry in her voice just made it worse. Weren't church people supposed to get happy endings from God? His twenty-four-hour venture into faith wasn't going very well, even though George had spouted some platitudes about God still being in control. "I'm more of a Motown guy than a heavy-metal one, but it seems I'm going to get chrome-plated tomorrow. I get fifteen whole hours at home before I have to report for surgery." The further he got into his explanation, the less it seemed worth the effort to keep the annoyance out of his voice.

"I'm sorry. I know that's not what you wanted." She hugged her arms. "You should never have stayed out there waiting for me."

He stopped, nearly losing one crutch in his effort to grab her elbow. "I don't regret it. Don't you think that for a second, Charlotte. I'm just mad I didn't get a clean getaway, that's all."

"You're going to be okay," she offered, even though she had no way of knowing that was true.

He simply nodded, not having a good comeback for that one.

Once they got him settled on his couch, George ticked off a list of instructions to Charlotte and bid goodbye with a promise to visit Jesse tomorrow at the hospital. "Make sure he calls his folks," George ordered on his way out the door.

Charlotte pulled an ottoman up to the couch. "Want me to get your cell phone?"

"No." He took her hand, pulling her in for another gentle kiss. "Not yet. How are you? Did you go back over there?"

She smiled and brushed the hair off his forehead. Her fingers were gentle and soothing. He wanted those hands nearby when he woke up from surgery tomorrow. He wanted those hands nearby every waking moment.

With a sort of slow-motion burst of light, he realized he loved her. Exclusively her, absolutely her.

"No. I slept most of the morning, and then Abby Reed came over to talk to me." Something bright danced in the corners of her eyes.

"That's nice." That struck him as a dumb response. "What'd she say?"

Charlotte took his hand in hers. It was much easier to push the pain out of his thoughts when she was near. "She offered me a job, Jesse. Evidently she's been thinking about expanding her business into a full-fledged yarn shop next door, but hadn't planned on doing it until the fall. When Melba told her this morning I was looking at a job in Vermont, Abby decided maybe it was time to speed up her time frame."

Jesse wished the pain medicine didn't sludge up his thinking so much. "A job? Here?"

The brightness in her eyes now lit up her whole face. "A job. Right here. We're still working out all the details but I think it's going to be perfect. I've always wanted to run a yarn shop—it's almost what I did with Mima's money. Now I can learn, only as part of another business and with a partner."

"Me?"

She laughed and slid off the ottoman to bring her face close to his. "No, silly, Abby. You'd be terrible as a yarn salesman."

He kissed her again, needing her close. "Nah, I'd be great." He reached up to touch her cheek. "You're staying."

She nodded. "I think so."

Maybe George's prayer army had pulled off getting him what he truly needed after all. "What about…us?"

He didn't think he could stand the thought of her being in Gordon Falls and not being with him. As he looked into her eyes, Jesse realized, with a crystal-clear shock of certainty, that he'd do whatever it took to be with her. Whatever it took. "I need us to be…us." He knew he wasn't being eloquent by a long shot, but the look in her eyes told him she understood. "Tell me what you need for that to happen." He'd never in his life placed someone else ahead of his own interests, never laid his own plans at the feet of someone else's needs. A fire rescue was one thing, but his whole life? How did that work? He was pretty sure faith was what made such a thing possible. Clark had said it before—even Charlotte had talked about it—but he'd never really believed it before now.

Jesse wanted to see certainty in her eyes, but saw honesty instead. She settled in against him, sitting on the floor and laying her head on his chest. "I don't know. At least not yet. I've got a lot of…baggage…in that department and I'm not sure how easy it will be to lay that all down."

"I'd leave it. The firehouse, I mean." He didn't even know that until it leaped from his mouth. He waited for the regret to come, but it didn't arrive. "It'd be hard, but I would."

A tender pain filled her face. "I don't want it to come to that. It's so much of who you are. I don't know what the answer is, but I have to think there is one out there."

For the first time, waiting didn't feel like procrastination. "We've got some time here. I'll be off duty for a while after the surgery." He grinned. "Look at me, all silver lining and stuff. Maybe God really is always right on time. This is going to take some getting used to. I've got authority issues."

Charlotte laughed, and Jesse felt the hum of it against his chest settle somewhere deep inside. "I've noticed." After a long spell of staring into his eyes, she ran one finger across his stubbled chin and whispered, "I love you. I don't know when it happened, but I'm glad it did."

The glow in his chest had nothing to do with any prescription. "I know when for me. I mean, I didn't at the time, but looking back, I know exactly the moment."

"You do?"

He nodded. "Berry cobbler." Just remembering the moment doubled the glow under his ribs.

"Then?"

"The face you made when you dug into it? A man can only take so much. I lost it right then and there. I didn't know it yet, but that was the end of it."

Her face flushed. "So that's why that kiss pulled the rug out from underneath me."

It had yanked him way off balance, too. "I didn't work it out, though, until the fire. I figured it was just a great kiss...until I thought maybe you were in that cottage. When that call came and I didn't know if you were safe... And then later when I thought about you driving back all that way all alone..."

She lay her hand across his chest, and he felt the warmth of her palm against his heartbeat. "Maybe that's what it took for both of us. All the stuff we thought we needed—lots of it is gone right now. Maybe that leaves more room for the stuff that really matters."

It was so clear, right then, what really mattered. He slid his arm around her shoulders and pulled her closer. "I love you. We'll work it out. Right here."

"On this couch?" Her laugh was soft and velvety against his cheek.

"It's a good place to start."

If he'd thought the kiss over the cobbler sealed his fate, he was dead wrong. The kiss she gave him now beat that one by a mile.

Epilogue

Ouch.

Jesse's head felt as if it had been stuffed with cement and he couldn't feel the tips of his fingers. His mouth was dry and something was beeping with annoying regularity off to his left. He forced his eyes open to a bright room.

"Hey there, hero."

It took him a minute to recognize the voice as Charlotte's. He rolled his head away from the beeping and saw her eyes in the glare.

"Welcome back."

He winced and grunted, no words coming beyond the dusty dryness of his mouth.

"Thirsty?"

He felt Charlotte's fingers feather across his forehead as he nodded.

She held a cup and straw up to let him drink, and he felt the cool water pull him back to life.

"You came through beautifully, Jesse. There's a plate in your leg now but it'll be okay."

Jesse recognized his mother's voice and turned his

head toward the foot of his bed, where his mother and father stood looking like twin parental pillars of worry.

"I always wanted to be in hardware," he choked out, the voice sounding as if it came down from the ceiling rather than from his own body.

"At the moment, you're in plastic. You get a fiberglass cast later." His father's voice filled the room, but without the edge it usually had. "You'll be back to your usual antics in a few weeks."

Not really. Jesse still hadn't figured out a way to tell his parents how drastically things had changed for him in just a matter of days. As he watched his mom's eyes dart back and forth between himself and Charlotte, it was clear she had caught on. Dad still looked a bit confused. "Maybe. Right now it hurts."

"I imagine it does."

"You always had a flair for the dramatic." Jesse turned to find Randy sitting on the guest chair. Randy was here. "Or should I say heroic?" He rose and offered Jesse his hand.

"That's me, your friendly neighborhood hero."

"That *is* you," Randy said, squeezing Jesse's hand. "You're pretty amazing. I may have to take back all my wisecracks about the firehouse." It was as close to a declaration of support as Jesse had ever gotten from Randy. "Let me know how I can help. I'll find the time." Jesse blinked hard, almost unsure he'd heard Randy correctly. The world really had been turning inside out lately.

"You will be off your feet for a while," Charlotte said. "George already has a schedule up at the firehouse for when your parents, Randy and I can't be there. And your church fan club will keep you in food clear through Thanksgiving if you need it."

"Why didn't you call us earlier?" His father's voice was tight with worry.

Jesse's first response was a knee-jerk "Why are you so concerned all of a sudden?" as the usual wound of his father's inattention roared to life. Only something made Jesse stop and look at his father's eyes rather than just react to his voice. He was genuinely concerned. It wasn't just the "Why do you do that firefighting thing?" Jesse always read into his father's inquiries. Today it looked more like "You were in danger." He wasn't quite sure what brought on the distinction. Had his father changed? Had even Randy changed? Or was it his ability to see his family that had altered?

An honest answer—instead of his usual wisecrack—came to him surprisingly easily. "I didn't really have time. And I knew I'd be okay."

"Oh, you knew, did you?" Mom did not look as though she shared that opinion. "Surgery is not my version of okay, son."

"I called you for the surgery part, Mom. And look at me, I'm fine." He wasn't fine—not yet, really—but he wanted that worried look to leave his mother's eyes. "Mom, Dad, Randy, this is Charlotte."

Charlotte laughed softly and his father smiled. "We had a chance to meet while you were getting your new hinges put in."

"So this is who bought the cottage," Dad said. His words hinted at more than a real estate transaction, and Jesse found himself wondering just how well his parents now knew his favorite customer. "I'm glad you weren't hurt in all that the other night."

"We have lots of work to do—" Jesse felt Charlotte's hand tighten on his "—but I think it will all work out in the end." She caught Jesse's eyes. The fact that she'd used the word *we* planted a grin on his face that had nothing to do with the postoperative painkillers.

Only he couldn't really help with the renovation work for now, could he? "Who are we going to get to help you finish the cottage?" He didn't really like the idea of anyone else working on that place—he liked to think of the project as his and Charlotte's alone.

"I think we can worry about that tomorrow. Chad Owens helped me call in a cleaning company that specializes in these things, and that will take a few days anyhow. And then there's all the insurance to be settled." She ran her thumb over the back of his palm and Jesse felt his eyes fall closed at the sensation. "We have time."

God is never late, and He's never early, Jesse thought as the fog began to fill his head again.

"What did you just say?" His father sounded baffled.

"It's something my grandmother taught me," he heard Charlotte's voice explain. "About how everything works out. 'God is never late, and He's never early. He's always right on time—His time.'"

"That's a lovely thought." His mother sounded pleased.

She's a lovely woman. I'm in love with her, Jesse thought to himself as he began to slip back asleep.

"You don't say?" Randy actually sounded amused. When had Randy learned to read minds?

"And I'm in love with you," he heard Charlotte whisper in his ear. "But we've got time for that, too."

"I think we'd better leave these two alone for a bit," came his mother's voice. "We'll meet you back here later to bring him home."

Jesse fought the fog to push his eyelids open. Charlotte had the sweetest look on her face. "I'm loopy," he admitted, realizing what had just happened. "But I still mean it." He brought his hand up to touch the delightful softness of her cheek. "I'm head over heels for you. Well, maybe just one heel at the moment."

She laughed. "One heel is enough. Though, I thought you were sweeping me off my feet, not the other way around." She parked one elbow on the bed beside him. "Your family is sweet. Your dad tries to hide it, but he's really worried about you. He cares, Jesse. He just isn't very good about knowing how to show it."

"I think they like you."

Her smile made his head spin. "I hope they do. I think they were onto us before your little pronouncement a moment ago."

"They'll have to get used to it sometime, why not now?" Jesse yawned and blinked. He needed her to know before he slipped away again. "I'm absolutely, one hundred and ten percent in love with you." The words were taking more effort to get out as the fog settled back in. "So you have to stay. You have to." He couldn't keep his eyes open any longer. "I need you. Stay, please?"

The last thing he remembered was the cool softness of her kiss on his forehead. "I know where home is now. I'm not going anywhere."

* * * * *

Dear Reader,

There is an old saying that "God laughs at our plans." I don't know that I believe that as much as I believe He smiles at *our* version of our plans, then gently remakes our striving into His better purpose. Sometimes not so gently, as many of us need a hefty shove to be headed in the right direction, yes? Jesse and Charlotte have dramatic turns in their lives, turns that pull them together but are by no means smooth transitions! I hope you draw faith for your own challenges from their story. If you'd like information on how to start a prayer shawl ministry at your church or just want to say hello, feel free to contact me at www.alliepleiter.com, "Like" me on Facebook or drop a line to P.O. Box 7026, Villa Park, IL 60181—I'd love to hear from you!

Allie Pleiter

Questions for Discussion

1. Would you have bought the cottage if you were in Charlotte's position? Why or why not?

2. Why is it that cautious people like Melba become friends with daring people like Charlotte? Has it been true in your life?

3. When have you had your plans yanked out from underneath you like Jesse has? What did you learn from it?

4. Do you have a "Mima" in your life? Are you a "Mima" to someone? Could you be?

5. Abby tells Charlotte she's got a "powerful posse of prayer warriors." Do you have people who pray for you regularly? If not, how could you create your own posse?

6. Are you a cat person or a dog person (or something else)?

7. Have you ever been drawn to a town the way Charlotte is drawn to Gordon Falls?

8. Is it a good thing to go full throttle at a project as Charlotte does on the cottage? Is there a wrong time to have that kind of enthusiasm? A right time?

9. What foods bring out your "piggish side"?

10. Was Charlotte wise to offer Jesse the chance to rent the cottage if she left?

11. Jesse uses his music to open himself up to faith. What first opened you up to faith?

12. When in your life have you needed consolation? How did it come to you?

13. Jesse says, "I couldn't help you from where I was, but I began to feel like God could." Have you ever found yourself in a situation like that?

14. Chief Bradens said he could always tell which people would beat the fire, and which people would let the fire beat them. Which do you think you are? How do you know?

15. Charlotte and the church ladies use their knitting to bless others. What gifts can you use to do the same?

REQUEST YOUR FREE BOOKS!

2 FREE INSPIRATIONAL NOVELS
PLUS 2
FREE
MYSTERY GIFTS

Love Inspired

YES! Please send me 2 FREE Love Inspired® novels and my 2 FREE mystery gifts (gifts are worth about $10). After receiving them, if I don't wish to receive any more books, I can return the shipping statement marked "cancel." If I don't cancel, I will receive 6 brand-new novels every month and be billed just $4.74 per book in the U.S. or $5.24 per book in Canada. That's a saving of at least 21% off the cover price. It's quite a bargain! Shipping and handling is just 50¢ per book in the U.S. and 75¢ per book in Canada.* I understand that accepting the 2 free books and gifts places me under no obligation to buy anything. I can always return a shipment and cancel at any time. Even if I never buy another book, the two free books and gifts are mine to keep forever.

105/305 IDN F47Y

Name _____ (PLEASE PRINT) _____

Address _____ Apt. # _____

City _____ State/Prov. _____ Zip/Postal Code _____

Signature (if under 18, a parent or guardian must sign) _____

Mail to the Harlequin® Reader Service:
IN U.S.A.: P.O. Box 1867, Buffalo, NY 14240-1867
IN CANADA: P.O. Box 609, Fort Erie, Ontario L2A 5X3

**Are you a subscriber to Love Inspired books
and want to receive the larger-print edition?
Call 1-800-873-8635 or visit www.ReaderService.com.**

* Terms and prices subject to change without notice. Prices do not include applicable taxes. Sales tax applicable in N.Y. Canadian residents will be charged applicable taxes. Offer not valid in Quebec. This offer is limited to one order per household. Not valid for current subscribers to Love Inspired books. All orders subject to credit approval. Credit or debit balances in a customer's account(s) may be offset by any other outstanding balance owed by or to the customer. Please allow 4 to 6 weeks for delivery. Offer available while quantities last.

Your Privacy—The Harlequin® Reader Service is committed to protecting your privacy. Our Privacy Policy is available online at www.ReaderService.com or upon request from the Harlequin Reader Service.

We make a portion of our mailing list available to reputable third parties that offer products we believe may interest you. If you prefer that we not exchange your name with third parties, or if you wish to clarify or modify your communication preferences, please visit us at www.ReaderService.com/consumerchoice or write to us at Harlequin Reader Service Preference Service, P.O. Box 9062, Buffalo, NY 14269. Include your complete name and address.

LI13R

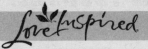
"Robin," Ethan said, just before his face appeared in the church belfry's open trapdoor, "come on up. It's perfectly safe."

He reached down a gloved hand as she put a foot on the bottom rung of the wrought-iron ladder.

"How does this thing work?"

"It's very simple. There's a tall pole with a hook on one end. I used it to slide open the trap and then pull down the ladder. When I'm done, I'll use it to push the ladder back up and lift it over the locking mechanism, then slide the trap closed."

"I see."

"Oh, you haven't seen anything yet," he told her, grasping her hand and all but lifting her up the last few rungs to stand next to him on a narrow metal platform. In their bulky coats, they had to stand pressed shoulder to shoulder. "Take a look at this." He swung his arm wide, encompassing the town, the valley beyond and the snow-capped mountains surrounding it all.

"Wow."

"Exactly," he said. "There's a part of Psalms 98 that says, 'Let the rivers clap their hands, let the mountains sing together for joy…' Seeing the view like this, you can almost feel it, can't you? The rivers and mountains praising their Creator."

"I never thought of rivers and mountains praising God," she admitted.

"Scripture speaks many times of nature praising God and testifying to His wonders."

"I can see why," she said reverently.

"So can I," he told her, smiling down at her with those warm brown eyes.

Her breath caught in her throat. But surely she was reading too much into that look. That wasn't appreciation she saw in his gaze. That was just her loneliness seeking connection. Wasn't it? Though she had never felt this sudden, electrical link before, as if something vital and masculine in him reached out and touched something fundamental and feminine in her. She had to be mistaken.

He was a man of God, after all.

Even if she couldn't help thinking of him as just a man.

*Will Robin and Ethan find love for Christmas,
or will her secrets stand in their way?
Find out in HER MONTANA CHRISTMAS
by Arlene James, available December 2014 wherever
Love Inspired® books and ebooks are sold.*

LIEXP1114

"Just tell me what happened to my daughter."

"We don't know. You were alone when we found you."

"I need to go home." Scout jumped up, head spinning,
the room spinning. The knot in her stomach growing until
it was all she could feel. "Maybe she's there."

She knew it was unreasonable, knew it couldn't be
true, but she had to look, had to be sure.

"The police have already been to your house," Boone
said gently. "She's not there."

"She could be hiding. She doesn't like strangers." Her
voice trembled. Her body trembled, every fear she'd ever
had, every nightmare, suddenly real and happening and
completely outside her control.

"Scout." He touched her shoulder, his fingers warm
through thin cotton. She didn't want warmth, though. She
wanted her child.

"Please," she begged. "I have to go home. I have to see
for myself. I have to."

He eyed her for a moment, silent. Solemn. Something
in his eyes that looked like the grief she was feeling, the
horror she was living.

Finally, Boone nodded. "Okay. I'll take you."

Just like that. Simple and easy, as if the request didn't

go against logic. As if she weren't hooked to an IV, shaking from fear and sorrow and pain.

He grabbed a blanket from the foot of the bed and wrapped it around her shoulders then took out his phone and texted someone. She didn't ask who. She was too busy trying to keep the darkness from taking her again. Too busy trying to remember the last moment she'd seen Lucy. Had she been scared? Crying?

Three days.

That was what he had said.

Three days that Lucy had been missing and Scout had been lying in a hospital bed.

Please, God, let her be okay.

She was all Scout had. The only thing that really mattered to her. She had to be okay.

A tear slipped down her cheek. She didn't have the energy to wipe it away. Didn't have the strength to even open her eyes when Boone touched her cheek.

"It's going to be okay," he said quietly, and she wanted to believe him almost as much as she wanted to open her eyes and see her daughter.

"How can it be?"

"Because you ran into the right person the night your daughter was taken," he responded, and he sounded so confident, so certain of the outcome, she looked into his face, his eyes. Saw those things she'd seen before, but something else, too—faith, passion, belief.

*Will Boone help Scout find her missing
daughter in time for Christmas?
Pick up HER CHRISTMAS GUARDIAN to find out!
Available December 2014
wherever Love Inspired® books and ebooks are sold.*